While Someone Watches

L A Walton

Copyright © 2015 L A Walton

All rights reserved.

ISBN: 151463760X
ISBN-13: 978-1514637609

DEDICATION

I'd like to dedicate this book to the very special people in my life. I couldn't do it without all of the love and support of my loving mother Estelle Walton and daughter Hannah Z. I also dedicate this book to my daily motivator who not only provides me with an overflow of inspiration, but has refused to let me ever give up. I dedicate this finally to the rest of my cheer section who have never left my side and have helped me to see the true value of friendship. Thank you. I love you all.

LAW

CHAPTER 1

"Hello my name is Marie Sa-"

"I'm sorry to interrupt you Marie but we don't use full names here on our Love Guru Shows. We actually try to use catchy nicknames like Restless with Relationships or Scary Style." Laci Cummings was talking into the microphone in front of her.

"Oh...I'm sorry. Then I want to be called Missing Marie."

"Missing Marie? This sounds serious."

"I do...I do have a serious question," Marie's voice was soft and barely audible.

"Well I'm here to help you Missing Marie. Ask when you're ready."

"I have a boyfriend. We've been dating for almost a year. He's handsome, has a good job, and he's really smart."

"Wow. He sounds like a keeper so far. Why am I sensing a 'but' is on the way?" Laci asked.

"He's wonderful...but he's also a little...controlling. He gets mad whenever I wear heels or skirts, he never lets me spend time with my family, and we had a huge fight yesterday about me having a Facebook account."

"Why did you have an argument over Facebook?"

"He didn't want me to have one and told me I had to deactivate my account. He said I was using it to flirt with other men."

"Are you?"

"No!"

"So what did you do?"

"I told him I would close my Facebook account."

Laci took a breath before speaking, "You closed your Facebook just because he told you to?".

"No, I told him I would close my Facebook but I didn't. I know relationships are about compromising but I feel like I'm the one that's constantly giving in to his jealousy. Am I wrong?"

"Well Missing Marie, I want to know if you feel safe with him."

"What do you mean?"

"Has he ever hurt you? Do you feel that he's capable of hurting you if you didn't listen to him? Do you feel safe with him? Is that maybe why you called yourself Missing Marie?"

"I...I don't know. Maybe."

"That's your answer," Laci whispered. "You should listen to your gut Marie. If he's acting this way, it normally won't get better unless he seeks help for his controlling behaviors."

"He hates therapists. He calls them whack jobs."

Laci laughed, "Well if he's not willing to see a whack job, what do you plan to do Marie?"

"I'm not sure if I can keep giving in to his demands. I think I'm going to have to break up with him. No...I will break up with him. There's nothing to think about. Right? We're done. When he comes over, I'll tell him we're through. I can do this."

"That's very brave of you Ms. Marie but I would suggest not breaking up in a private place if he is controlling. It may be safer for you to break up in a public place where there are a lot of people around."

"No! I have to do it tonight before I chicken out. Thanks Laci."

"Marie listen to me. Hello?" Laci looked over to her producer, George. He signaled that the caller had left the chat room.

"Well...it seems Missing Marie found courage to stand up to someone who might do her harm, but I really hope you stay safe and make wise choices tonight Marie. Our show is almost done, so as usual, I wanted to read you a letter from one of our listeners. This is from Stitching Hurt.

'Dear Laci,
I chatted with you last year because I was in an abusive relationship. My guy was smart, handsome, and rich but he was also controlling and then he became abusive. Thanks to you, I was able to escape from him. Now I'm in a better relationship and I'm about to get married. I owe it all to you. Thank you. From the bottom of my heart I thank you. I truly believe that if I had stayed with him, I would be dead right now. Come to my wedding! Please come to my wedding!
-Stitching Hurt

I'm happy for you Stitching Hurt, and I would love to come to your wedding. Missing Marie wherever you are...please be safe tonight. That's it folks. From us here at Love Guru, we're wishing you sweet dreams East Coast. Remember if you ask us, we will help you find the answer."

"If you ask us, we will help you find the answer."

"Witch," he muttered under his breath as he clicked the button to switch off his XM Radio. He recognized the voice of the woman who called herself Missing Marie. That was his Marie. Marie Sanchez. "She wants to break up with me? I don't think so."

He knew Marie listened to Love Guru on a daily basis. His last girlfriend listened to Laci Cummings as well. Monday through Friday this idiot that women called the *"Woman Whisperer"* and *"Love Guru"* when it came to everything from fashion to relationships and would give out advice on all topics via the XM talk show and ran a very successful magazine called Modern Self that she has recently sold so she could just write advice columns and give advice with her own XM talk show. As far as he was concerned, she didn't have a clue about relationships.

He drove up to the yellow two story house and let himself in with the key Marie had given him a few months prior.

"Hey you're here early," she said once she saw him. He noticed that she didn't come and kiss him as she normally did. Come to think of it, she hadn't been doing that for a couple of weeks now.

"Anything exciting happen today?" he asked as he took off his jacket.

"No. Nothing too exciting. After dinner, I think there's something we need to talk about."

"Is it important?"

She was nervous. He could tell because she kept pulling on her left ear. "A little," she whispered.

"I'm sorry, I didn't hear you."

"Nothing. I forgot I left my phone upstairs. I'll be right back." She started to walk up the stairs when he began following her. She looked over her shoulder, "You don't have to follow me. I'll be right down."

He smiled, "I know babe, and I want to follow you."

She tugged her left ear again, "Umm...okay."

He followed her into her bedroom. He could see his picture on her bedside table. He didn't understand why she would want to break up with him if she had really loved him. It had to be Laci Cumming's fault. It had to be.

"Listen, maybe we shouldn't wait until after dinner. This is important."

He stood in front of her and placed his hands on both of her shoulders, "Babe, whatever it is...we can work it out. You look scared. What's going on?"

She shrugged her shoulders, "I just feel like lately you've been very demanding."

"Demanding? How so?"

"Don't get mad...but like how you're always telling me not to wear dresses or makeup. How I can't go out with my friends or sisters. You didn't even want me to have a Facebook account!"

"I see. So you think your boyfriend not wanting you to dress like a skank, hang out with skanks, or talk on the Internet like a skank is bad."

"What are you talking about? When have I ever dressed like a skank?"

"Marie why don't you just say what you want to say?"

"I want to break up!"

There was a moment of silence after she yelled it. He stared at her and she felt uncomfortable. They were standing in her bedroom and she needed to escape. She felt trapped with him...like he was a ticking time bomb.

"Don't worry. I'm not mad."

She was surprised by his words, "What?"

He looked up at her and smiled, "I'm not mad. I'm actually kind of relieved."

"You're relieved? I don't understand."

"Marie...I've been wanting to call it quits for a few weeks now but I didn't know how to tell you. I thought if I started acting like a jerk you would dump me but you didn't. Then I felt guilty because you must've really loved me to put up with me."

"What? Wait...what?" Marie was running her hands in through her hair in confusion. "I'm not understanding. You wanted me to dump you?"

"Yes."

"Why?"

He was mentally laughing. She wanted to dump him but as soon as she found out he wanted to be dumped, she was upset.

"Does it matter why? We both want the same thing." He turned to leave the bedroom when she grabbed his arm.

"Wait a minute. We didn't want the same thing. I only wanted to dump you because you were being possessive. If that was an act, I have a right to know why you didn't want to date me."

"So if I'm not being possessive or demanding, you would want to continue dating me?" he asked.

She looked confused at everything that was

happening and then nodded, "Yes. Yes I would."

He sighed heavily, "Fine. Let's try to make this work then."

"Fine," she said a little too forcefully. "Let's go have dinner then."

She walked ahead of him and headed to the stairs.

"Marie?"

She looked over her shoulder at him, "Yeah?"

"So if I hadn't been acting...you would've really broken up with me?"

She smiled and scrunched her nose, "Of course. You were acting like a goat. Thank God you were just pretending."

He nodded and placed his hands on her shoulders and began massaging them as they walked, "Yeah, thank Goodness."

He kissed her on the forehead and whispered, "I love you."

She was still confused, "So why did you want to break up with me? If you love me...why the big act?"

"Marie you're so beautiful but so slow sometimes."

"What?"

"I never wanted to break up with you."

"Then why were you acting like an obsessive jerk?"

He leaned in and kissed her cheek before whispering in her ear, "Because I am an obsessive jerk...and I wasn't acting."

Before she could respond, he shoved her down the stairs. It happened so quickly that she didn't have time to grab onto anything. She just stumbled down the steps. He heard a bone cracking. He stood there at the top of the stairs, her body contorted at the bottom. Her neck was at a weird angle...clearly broken.

He slowly walked down the stairs and took a long step over her body. "Tsk tsk Marie. You shouldn't be so clumsy." He pulled her cell phone out of her hand and deleted her call to Love Guru.

He took out his cell phone and dialed 911. In a voice filled with panic he responded to the operator, "Oh God, my girlfriend jut fell down the stairs. Please help her. Oh God please help her now."

He looked over to Marie's now dead body and smiled. She wasn't his first victim and she wouldn't be his last.

CHAPTER 2

Laci Cummings was checking her e-mail when her phone rang.

"This is Laci, talk to me."

"Laci ...where the heck are you?"

"At home. Where else would I be? I'm all work and no play." She recognized the voice. It was her producer George.

"You were supposed to be at the station this morning. Remember we had an important meeting?"

Laci turned her head to look at the calendar on her wall. The day was circled in red. "Aw crap. I forgot. Okay give me fifteen minutes and I'll be there."

"I'll give you ten and your golden tush better be sitting in one of these pleather chairs ASAP! I don't get paid as much as you do doll!"

"Thirty minutes. I got it! Thanks George. You're a peach." Before he could repeat that she only had ten minutes, she hung up the phone and grabbed her big black purse. She fished out her car keys and ran outside to her white Mercedes.

After stopping by Starbucks and picking up a mocha latte, she made her way through the radio station's lobby. The building was actually a large media hub that housed a local news station, the magazine, as well as a recording studio. As she passed the security guard, Laci raised her hand, "Hey Eric!"

"Hola Dr. Cummings!" he waved back.

She was humming the tune to a Taylor Swift song that somehow got stuck in her head back at Starbucks when the elevator opened. She got inside and pressed the button for the fifth floor. The door was about to close when someone suddenly stuck their hand in between the doors.

An athletic build of a man that looked like he stepped out of the Gangster Squad movie, complete with suspenders and hat, brown hair with matching brown eyes smiled at her, "So sorry but I'm already late."

Laci laughed, "Join the club."

He looked at the buttons on the elevator, "What a coincidence. We're heading to the same floor."

Laci smiled, "Do you work there? I've never seen you before." Especially with a look like that, thinking to herself.

He stuck out his hand, "Andrew. Dr. Andrew Brett."

Laci shook his hand as the elevator opened again, "Well here we are."

They both walked to the station manager's office. Laci thought it was strange that he was heading in the same direction as her. When she knocked on his door, Simpson, the station manager looked up and smiled. "So the two of you already met. Fantastic."

George stood up with a confused look on his face. "You two already know each other?"

"Yeah for all of five seconds. We just met on the elevator."

Simpson's expression fell, "Oh well then, George has something important to tell you."

"She doesn't know?" Andrew asked.

"Know what?"

Andrew looked at Simpson and George who were conveniently looking at their shoes and phone. He sighed, "I'm going to be your new partner on Love Guru."

"What the heck? You couldn't warn me?" Laci was livid. She didn't even get to finish drinking her latte which made her even more upset. She eyed both men to see if she threw it at them which one she would hit.

"We want to reach a male demographic that we haven't been able to hit just yet," George explained.

"A male demographic? Men don't listen to relationship advice radio shows," Laci began pacing in Simpson's office.

"Exactly!" Simpson also stood up, "Andrew is hip and cool. Men can look up to him and take his advice especially now since he's the
new editor of Modern Self....I probably could have picked another time to mention that."

"WHAT?! They chose a MAN to run the magazine?!" Laci looked over at Andrew. "No offense, I'm sure you are a pretty decent guy."

Andrew, who was finding this all quite amusing, tipped his hat, and gave her a wink, "Why thank you Laci, I very much appreciate the compliment."

Laci rolled her eyes, "First of all Simpson...no one and I do mean no one says 'hip and cool' anymore. Second, are you trying to replace me?"

"No!" they both said in unison.

"We want you two to work together," Simpson explained. "He used to have a radio show in Boston that did really well but he quit to focus on his personal clients and his self-help books. He's been living here in Atlanta, and when we found out he took the job as the new editor of Modern Self, we lured him to be on the show. I didn't tell you about it because I knew you'd be ticked. We weren't even sure he would agree but he did."

"So now what happens?" Laci asked.

"Now you do the show together. If it flops, things go back to the way they were...but I'm hoping that this works out well Laci." Simpson shot her a death stare as if she would purposely sabotage the new guy.

"Fine. I'll do the show with him but if he doesn't work out we go back to how things were."

"That's all we're asking," Simpson smiled.

Laci gave him the stink eye before exiting his office. She looked at Andrew who was leaning against the wall with his hands in his pockets like he didn't have a care in the world.

"Follow me Mr. Male Demographic," Laci motioned for him to follow.

"I'm sorry what did you say?"

"I said to follow me. I'll show you around."

Laci spent the morning introducing Andrew to the different staff members. When they were done, she gave him a rundown of how her show worked. "I usually give advice and answer questions. At the end of the show I like to read a random letter from a listener."

"Do you pick the letter?"

"No, I let George choose whatever. It doesn't really matter to me."

"Sounds easy enough," Andrew said as he was trying to keep up with her. "So what are we going to do to liven up the show?"

"What do you mean?"

"Well I was brought here for a reason. We need to reach men and reading letters isn't going to do it."

Laci counted to five in her head before responding, "Okay...what do you suggest?"

"Hmmm...I don't know something like a he said she said segment."

"He said she said?"

"Yeah like we each give opposing points of view on a topic and then let the listeners call in and pick sides." He smiled at Laci and she couldn't help but smile back.

"Sounds good. We'll try it. You pick the topic though."

"Why me?"

"Why not?"

He smiled at her cheekiness. "Okay, I'll pick the topic. I'm choosing harassment."

"Harassment?" Laci asked.

"Yeah. When a cute guy hits on a woman it's flirting but when an ugly guy hits on a woman it's harassment."

Laci laughed, "How are you going to argue that? Like any woman would ever consider you ugly."

Andrew smiled, "Why Dr. Cummings, are you calling me handsome?" He tilted his head just enough to peer from under his hat.

"I think I need the number to HR. What does that tell you?"

He laughed as she walked off holding up her cold latte in goodbye.

"This is going to be fun," he whispered to himself.

"Laci. Laci. Laci!"

"I'm coming! Calm down!" Laci ran to her door and opened it to see her brother Declan Cummings.

"Declan!" Laci hugged her brother tightly then pushed him away and punched him in the stomach. "You prick! I've been trying to get in touch with you for weeks. Where the heck were you?"

"On sabbatical."

Laci scoffed, "More like with a bunch of skanks somewhere."

Declan laughed, "Sis' I am a mature young man now. I wouldn't do such a thing."

"Riiight and I'm Santa Claus."

"Wait. What? You're Santa Claus? Can I tell you what I want for Christmas?"

Laci punched him in the arm, "Sorry Declan. Santa says 'ho ho ho' but he doesn't deliver them."

"Ha ha...not funny. So are you, the almighty woman whisperer and big sister, gonna let me stay with you for a few weeks?"

"Hmmm...I don't know. Do I really want an annoying brother living with me?"

"Annoying?" Declan pretended to be offended which made Laci laugh.

"Of course you can stay with me. You don't even have to ask. Just don't bother my clients when they come over."

"You have clients come here? Is that even safe?"

Laci laughed, "Knock on wood brother. I haven't

had any problems yet."

"You're in the right field I guess. You have to be wacked to help the wacked."

"Henry! Where are you Henry?"

Henry sat in his closet, trying to be quiet. He just wanted some peace and quiet. Suddenly the door opened, and there stood his wife, Portia. She gave him a disgusted look. "Are you hiding in the closet Henry?"

"Uh...no."

"Really? Then what are you doing?"

"I'm looking for my slippers."

"If you're looking for your slippers, why are you sitting down in a dark closet?"

"I don't know."

Portia rolled her eyes and shook her head, "Forget it. I don't want to know. I just wanted to tell you that I confirmed our appointment with Dr.Cummings tomorrow."

"Great," Henry smiled.

Portia sighed, "I should've listened to my mother and married a doctor." She turned around and left Henry alone in his closet.

He smiled, "Dr. Cummings." He got up and walked to his dresser drawer which he kept locked. He opened up a small journal that he kept hidden from his wife. He flipped through the pages. Inside were hand drawings of Dr. Cummings. He looked around to make sure Portia wasn't around and whispered, "I'll see you tomorrow my love."

CHAPTER 3

"So, Dr. Brett…what you are suggesting is that women are phony beings that only get upset when unattractive men hit on them." Dr. Laci Cummings was holding back a smile as she talked into her microphone.

He laughed. "No…I'm not saying that Laci. What I'm saying is that it's a well-known stereotype that women often overlook a man's advances as harassment if he is considered good looking."

"So if someone good looking like Ryan Gosling were to hit on me…I would be fine with it but if someone who looked like Mr. Bean asked me out, I would be dialing Human Resources?"

"According to the stereotype…yes."

"Well ladies and gentlemen, what do you think? Is the stereotype true or total BS?"

George, the producer signaled that they had a female caller on the line. Laci picked it up, "Well hello there you're live on Love Guru with doctors Brett and Cummings."

"Hi this is Meg."

"Hi there Meg," Andrew was going to take the call instead of Laci.

"Hi Dr. Brett. Can I just say that you two are wonderful together! I listen to the show every night and today has been amazing. I can't wait for them to put your face on the website so we can see what you look like."

Andrew laughed. "Oh no…I hope I don't disappoint you."

Laci piped in, "Meg don't worry. He's incredibly handsome."

Andrew smiled and Laci could have sworn he was blushing before he moved on, "So Meg…who do you think is right? Me or Laci?"

"Well…I think Dr. Brett is right. I had a creepy guy hit on me at work and I complained about him but if he had been better looking, I probably wouldn't have minded." Meg began giggling on the phone.

"For shame Meg! How could you go against your fellow females?" Laci laughed.

George signaled that another caller was on the line, "Love Guru, you're on the air," Andrew said.

"Hi my name is Keith."

"Hi Keith," they both said at the same time.

"I think Dr. Brett is right too. Women only want to date good looking guys."

"Whoa Keith," Laci interrupted, "Couldn't you say the same for men? Are you honestly going to say you wouldn't rather date a beautiful woman over an unattractive one?"

"Well a woman is a woman so it wouldn't matter to me," Keith said.

"Thank you for your support Keith. It means a lot

to know that both women and men think I'm right and Laci is wrong." Andrew was laughing as Laci gave him the stink eye.

"Fine. If we're going to talk about stereotypes, then I guess it wouldn't matter if we switched the roles and had a woman hitting on a male employee. According to your logic, men would never complain because they'll go after anything with two legs."

"Harsh!" Andrew said into his microphone, "Men can you believe this beautiful lady just said that? What do you have to say in defense?"

George signaled another caller. Andrew welcomed the caller, "Love Guru, you're live."

"It's me again. Keith."

Laci laughed, "Hi Keith."

"I just wanted to say that I agree with Dr. Cummings. I would also like to know if she would give me her number. She sounds hot."

Both Andrew and Laci started laughing. "I'm sorry Keith but she's too beautiful to not have a boyfriend so I don't think you'll be getting her number."

George signaled that time was almost up and to read the last letter of the day.

"Alright everyone, it's time to wrap it up so as usual we'll end the day with a letter from one of our listeners. This was actually an e-mail that was sent to us." Laci pulled out the letter and handed it to Andrew, "Would you like to read it Dr. Brett?"

"Sure. Okay here goes," he cleared his throat and read the letter.

"Dear Dr. Cummings,

I have listened to your show on and off for the past two years. I only listen because my past girlfriends have all loved your show. My last girlfriend felt I was too controlling and she broke up with me. So that this doesn't happen again, I'm going to start listening to your show religiously. I'll be listening to your every word. I won't miss a single syllable that comes out of your mouth. I'll be like an animal that stalks his prey. I'm going to learn everything there is to know about being in a relationship so that I can finally find my soul mate. Faithfully listening – Your Nightly Hunter."

"Wow," Laci wasn't sure how to respond to that message.

"Well Nightly Hunter," Andrew said as he scanned the e-mail again, "I would advise you to never ever send a woman a letter saying that you'll be like an animal that stalks his prey. In fact I wouldn't be surprised if the cops show up at your home tonight bud."

Laci laughed at Andrew's attempt to lighten the mood. "We get all kinds here at Love Guru. Our Motto is as us anything."

After the show was over, Laci stormed into George's booth. "What the heck was that George?"

"I'm sorry Laci, I didn't get a chance to read it over. We've never gotten creepy letters like that before. It won't happen again."

"Forget it. It was just a little weird. To compare himself to an animal that stalks its prey apparently means he wants to get close to me," Laci muttered to herself.

"You know I hate when your shrinky side comes out. That is why I think you're single, you're always trying to analyze people. I love that you do it more secretly that other shrinky people like you, but sometimes you just let it out. Just forget about it Laci. He was some crazed crackpot, that's all."

Andrew didn't agree, "Just be careful Laci. I agree with you that comparing himself to a stalker type animal indicates he wants to form some sort of intimate connection with you."

"Wow! He does it too. Great, now I got two shrinky dink people to deal with," George said and shook his head, "Anyway, you did great Andrew. Absolutely amazing! You two have incredible chemistry. I bet people are going to come up with cute names for you two like Shrinky Dink or…I can't think of another one."

"And on that note, I'm out of here. My brother is waiting for me so have a good night everyone. Andrew, you did great. I enjoyed working with you. I'll see you on Monday."

Laci waved her hand in the air as George stopped Andrew to talk about eating out in celebration of his new role on the show.

"Shouldn't we invite Laci?" Andrew asked.

George laughed, "No. I already told her she was uninvited. No women allowed. C'mon let's go."

"So brother, what did you do tonight?" Declan was stuffing popcorn in his mouth, "I watched movies."

"You didn't listen to my show?"

"Oh heck no! Why would I want to listen to all that

girly talk?"

"It's not girly talk! Besides I have a male co-host now."

"Ooooh….let me set my alarm for the next time your show plays," Declan said sarcastically.

Laci laughed and hit him playfully with her magazine, "Bad brother."

They both laughed at each other. "So what's the plan this weekend?" Declan was still eating his popcorn as he looked at Laci expectantly.

"The plan?"

"Yeah. What are we going to do?"

"I don't know about you…but I'm going to work. I have a few clients coming in."

"Are you serious? You're having coconuts coming over the weekend?"

"They're not coconuts. They're my clients Declan."

"Well, excuse 'em wee wee"

"That's not how the saying goes," Laci laughed.

"I missed you Laci."

Laci hugged her brother as they both sat on the sofa, "I missed you too Declan."

"Can you imagine how we would've ended up if we hadn't been adopted?"

"No, I can't imagine it at all," Laci sighed. Growing up she was bounced around from foster home to foster home until she was adopted at the incredibly old age of ten. By foster care standards, that was old. Her adoptive parents were Lisa and David Cummings. They had adopted Laci and then Declan two years later. It was an instant family connection between the two of them. The few people who found out that they weren't blood related were always surprised to find out that they were adopted because of their closeness.

"I miss mom and dad too," Declan whispered.

Lisa and David Cummings had passed away a few years ago, leaving Declan and Laci to carry on the family without them. The two always tried to spend major holidays together but Declan was always traveling and Laci was always working.

"Me too," Laci whispered.

"So what do you want to do tonight?"

"Sleep," Laci laughed.

"C'mon. Let's go somewhere. It's boring here," Declan whined.

"Gee thanks."

"You know what I mean."

Declan was an adventurer so staying at home was the worst sort of way to spend the evening. Laci was about to suggest they go see a movie when her phone rang.

"Hello?"

"Laci?"

"This is she. Who is this?"

"It's me Andrew. Sorry for just calling you but I got your number from George's phone. Can you please help me out?"

Laci laughed, "Which strip club?"

"How did you know?"

"You went out with George, right? He always wants to go to a strip club. He'll end up sloppy drunk and won't be able to get himself home."

"Why didn't you warn me?"

"It's your initiation," Laci laughed. Andrew told her where he and George were at so that she could pick them up. After she hung up, she turned to her brother, "So bro...you wanna go to a strip club?"

"Never in my life would I ever imagine my sister saying that to me," Declan said, "Nor could I imagine myself answering as I'm about to."

"You don't want to go?"

"No. My answer is heck yeah sister, let's hit that strip joint!"

"You're disgusting."

"I don't deny it." Declan grabbed his jacket and the two of them headed off into the Atlanta night.

"This place is disgusting," Laci grimaced as she walked in with Declan to meet Andrew and George.

"Oooh they have a fish buffet," Declan was about to make himself a shrimp plate when Laci stopped him, "Don't even think about it. Who knows what diseases that food has?"

"You worry too much."

"Here are the keys," Laci handed him the keys, "Go bring the car upfront."

"Fine. I never get to have any fun," Declan pretended to pout like a kid, making Laci laugh. She spotted George and Andrew. George was getting a lap dance from a woman that resembled Elsa from the Frozen movie. Well…if Elsa was a disgusting pot head. She waved at Andrew who tried picking George up. He had to give the blonde headed stripper some bills before she walked away.

"Thank you for coming," Andrew said.

"No problem. Do you have his keys?"

"Yeah."

"Why don't you bring the car around and I'll wait here with George."

"Okay, I'll be right back."

"Laci!"

Laci turned around to see Declan back inside the

strip club. "I thought you were waiting outside."

"I already brought the car out front. Did you need help bringing him outside?"

"Good thinking. Let's go."

Declan helped walk the tipsy George outside into the fresh air. Andrew was pulling up in George's car.

"I guess we'll follow you and then take you back to the station so that you can pick up your car." Laci said.

"Okay sounds good. Thanks again Laci." Andrew smiled from behind George's SUV. They all struggled to get George in his car.

"No I don't want to go. I want Elsa." George slurred.

"Don't ever let me get this drunk Laci," Declan whispered to her.

"No one should ever get this drunk," she whispered back.

After they got George inside the passenger side of his SUV, Laci walked back to her car with Declan in tow.

"What's that?" she asked.

"What's what?" Declan looked in the direction her index finger was pointing. Behind her windshield wiper was a small gold envelope.

"What the... That wasn't there when I parked a few minutes ago," Declan said.

As they got closer to the car, he pulled out the gold envelope from the windshield wiper and opened it, There's a letter inside."   A chill suddenly went down Laci's spine.

CHAPTER 4

"Are you okay Laci? You've been acting weird since we left off that Andrew guy." Declan was pulling a water bottle from the refrigerator.

Laci was sitting at the kitchen table, "He's Dr. Brett and I'm fine Declan. I'm just tired."

Declan nodded, "Are you freaked out about that note? I'm telling you it probably wasn't for you. Some drunk person more than likely thought it was for one of those strippers."

Laci smiled, "Is my brother worried? I do believe he is. Awww thank you baby brother."

Declan flicked her off, making her laugh.

"Seriously, are you okay?" he asked.

"Yes. I'm fine. It was just weird…that's all."

"You going to sleep okay?"

"My Tylenol PMs will ensure it."

"That's my sister…the pill popper," Declan smiled and ruffled her hair as he walked past her to go to his bedroom and call it a night.

Laci checked the doors to make sure they were

locked and then turned off the lights. It was a nightly ritual for her. Check the locks on the doors and windows and then turn off the lights. Then she could sleep in peace.

She walked to her bedroom and flipped on her laptop. She needed to check her e-mails for her advice column that she wrote for the local newspaper. She had clicked opened her e-mail account and smiled. She had over a hundred messages. It felt good to be popular. She clicked open the first message.

"Dear Laci,
My boyfriend thinks it's okay to keep talking to his ex on Facebook. She's always interfering in our relationship because she knows what's going on with his life. Should I ask him to delete her as a friend or should I just delete him as a boyfriend? —Fed up with Facebook"

Laci chuckled, "What's up with relationships having problems with Facebook these days?"

She typed her response.

"Dear Fed up,
Your insecurities about your boyfriend speaking with his ex should be discussed with him. Everyone has baggage but if he's unwilling to let go of his, you may have a problem. Evaluate your relationship after you speak with him about how you feel. If you're contemplating ending the relationship, it sounds like you may already have your answer. Follow your gut not your heart. –Laci"

Laci clicked on the next question.

"Dear Laci,
I've been dating "Jack" for three months now and he said its way past time for me to have sex with him. I'm still not ready but if I don't sleep with him I'm afraid he'll break up with me. What should I do? – Scared of Sex"

"Dear Scared,
I'm going to take a shot in the dark and guess that you're still a teenager. Even if you aren't the advice is still the same. Your body is YOUR BODY! No one should make you do anything you don't want to do. If "Tom" is pressuring you to have sex and you don't want to, he needs to respect that. If you don't feel ready, there's a reason for it. It's because…you're NOT ready! If Tom dumps you, then let him go. I'm not saying it will be easy…it may be very hard but so is living with the regret that you gave yourself to the wrong person. If you are a teenager, I would also suggest talking to an adult you're close to like a parent or visiting a free Health Clinic because I as I hope you know, having intercourse leads to having babies."

Laci clicked on her next e-mail. It was actually an e-card. It had a picture of a cute cartoon porcupine with binoculars and the caption, "Don't forget." She opened the e-card and music started playing. She turned up her speakers. It was a song from the 80's by Rockwell featuring Michael Jackson. It was titled Somebody's Watching Me.

As they lyrics played, she couldn't help but feel a shudder run down her spine, "Somebody's watching me? Great. It's the perfect scare tactic for a stalker." She flipped off her computer and took a deep breath. She wasn't sure if it was a string of coincidences or if it was the same person sending her messages but for now she was going to ignore it and hope that it stopped. If it didn't, she was going to have to get the authorities involved.

"Declan, I have some clients coming over today so make yourself scarce. Got it?"

"I still can't believe you let them know where you live," Declan said shaking his head in disbelief.

"Believe it or not, many psychologists and therapists treat clients out of their homes."

"Yeah…because they need to see a therapist themselves. You'd have to be crazy to let these people know where you live."

"Declan. These are couples looking for couple's therapy…not clients that have mental illnesses."

"So if you're married, you can't have schizophrenia? Is that what you're saying?"

Laci gave him the stink eye, "Shut up. You know what I mean. Now go find something to do for an hour or two."

"Are you sure you don't want me to stay in case they get too rowdy? I could be your personal bouncer or something. I'll kick them out if they start fighting."

"Go!" Laci was pushing a laughing Declan out the door.

Fifteen minutes later, Laci' doorbell was ringing. It was Portia and Henry Meiser. Laci greeted them and brought them into her study which she used as her office to see clients in.

"Dr. Cummings. He's doing it again! He's been hiding in the closet." Portia was sitting as far away from Henry as she could.

Laci took in Henry's wrinkled shirt and jeans. He was a stark contrast to Portia's pressed dress and heels. Laci wasn't sure but she thought he even had a ketchup stain on his collar.

"Henry, is that true?"

Henry looked uncomfortable and fidgeted in his seat. He didn't want to admit to doing something embarrassing.

"Just tell her Henry! You like to hide in closets. Dr. Cummings," Portia put her hand up to shield her mouth and whispered, "Do you think this means Henry is secretly gay?"

"What?" Henry shot a quick glance to Dr. Cummings before chastising his wife, "I'm not gay Portia!"

Portia shrugged her shoulders.

"Portia," Dr. Cummings smiled, "Can you tell us what made you fall in love with Henry in the first place?"

"Hmmm...I don't remember really. He used to make me laugh all of the time and he was smart. He always was always a gentleman."

"That sounds great Portia. What about you Henry? What made you fall in love with Portia?"

Henry looked at his wife who was preening in front of him. "Well she's beautiful. She used to be really kind before we got rich…then she changed."

"Changed? How did I change Henry?"

Laci cut them off before they began arguing again. She had watched them argue enough to learn their patterns and didn't need to witness anymore. "I'm going to give you each a journal to write in."

They both took a journal as Laci explained what they were to do with the journals. Then they discussed spending more time together. "I want you two to do activities together. Start rebuilding the emotional bond you two once had."

Laci listened to them decide to take an art class together. "That sounds great!"

After the couple left Laci texted her brother to come back home. Her phone rang and she thought it was going to be Declan but instead it was Amber, one of her best friends.

"Hey Freckles, are you coming to meet with us for lunch today?" Amber asked.

"Who's going to be there?"

Amber laughed, "The usual. You, me, Marie Ann, and Kay."

"Where are we meeting?"

"The Chinese Chopsticks. Kay keeps asking to eat there."

"Okay sounds good. I'll see you in twenty."

Laci sent a text to Declan that she would be out and quickly got ready to meet with her friends.

"So? Who's the sexy sounding Dr. Brett on your show?" Kay asked.

Laci blushed, "He's Andrew Brett and he's a colleague. Nothing more."

"Yet," Marie Ann chimed in. They all started laughing. Laci had been having lunch with these girls for years. They had all become friends in college.

Laci' phone dinged and she checked her message. It was from her brother.

"What the hay??? You went to have lunch without me? What kind of big sister are you?"

The text caused Laci to laugh because she knew that her brother was joking. She looked at the women around her and asked, "Oh did I tell you all? My brother is back in town!"

"What! When are we finally going to meet him?" Amber asked.

"I don't know. He might end up hitting on one of you and that would be awkward."

Kay laughed, "Is he cute?"

"He's my brother but even I will admit that he's handsome. I mean really handsome."

"Where was he?" Marie Ann asked as she took a sip of her sweet tea.

"He wouldn't tell me. He can work from wherever since he's a freelance graphic designer but he wouldn't even give me a clue."

"That's weird. You're his sister," Amber said.

"Tell me about it. I'm afraid he secretly knocked some girl up and doesn't want to admit it to me. Ladies, I love my brother…but he's a player."

They all started laughing.

"So does he not have a steady income?" Kay asked.

Laci raised her brow, "Please don't tell me you're actually interested in meeting my brother."

Kay raised her hands in defense, "What? He's

single...I'm single."

"He makes good money. A lot of companies want him to become a steady employee with them but he likes to travel too much to stop doing freelance. If you can get him to settle down, I would love it."

They all started laughing as their lunch was being brought to them.

In a corner of the Chinese Chopsticks sat a man who was staring at four women having lunch. He hadn't expected to see them there but what a wonderful surprise it turned out to be. He was close enough to listen to their conversations. He learned their names: Amber, Kay, Marie Ann, and of course Laci Cummings. She was the woman that would have to be taught a lesson. He flagged the waitress and asked for his meal to go along with the check. As she brought his food in a Styrofoam box, he stood up quietly, not wanting to be noticed by the four women. He went to pay and as he did so, he wrote a quick note on the back of a napkin. He asked that it be passed to the table that the four women were at. The cashier nodded and after the man had left she passed it to one of the waitresses.

"Excuse me, is there a Laci at this table?"

The four women looked up in surprise.

"I'm Laci. Is there a problem?"

"A customer that left asked that we give this to you?"

"Me?"

The waitress nodded.

Laci read the note and paled.

"What's wrong Laci?" Amber asked.

Laci flagged the waitress and asked her, "The customer that gave you this...what did he look like?"

The waitress shrugged, "I don't know. I didn't see him. I'll ask the cashier." She quickly left and then came back. "I'm sorry she doesn't remember. All she said was that he had dark hair."

"Well that helps a whole bunch," Kay said sarcastically. "What does the note say Laci?"

Laci shook her head and stuck the note in her purse. "It's just a fan, that's all. Hey Kay are you going to eat that biscuit?"

The girls weren't sure whether to let it drop but they did once Kay answered, "No. I don't need to be eating anymore carbs as it is. Take it from me you heifer."

After lunch was over, Laci sat in her car and pulled out the napkin. She thought of the e-card she had gotten earlier and sighed. The note had to be from the same person. So much for being a nightly hunter. It was lunch time and she was getting creepy notes. The lyrics from another popular 80s song, this time it was Welcome to the Jungle by Guns n Roses, were right in front of her as she read the note again and the last line was underlined.

Welcome to the jungle
It gets worse here everyday
You learn to live like an animal
In the jungle where we play
Welcome to the jungle
Watch it bring you to your knees
<u>I'm gonna watch you bleed</u>

CHAPTER 5

"So this is the napkin they gave you in the restaurant?" Officer Joe Bishop asked Laci as she sat to the side of his desk at the local police station.

"Yes. I think he's been stalking me."

"Stalking you?"

"Yes, stalking me. I got an e-mail with the song from Michael Jackson. It's the lyrics to Somebody's Watching Me."

Officer Bishop sighed as he placed the napkin on his desk, "Listen Ms. Cummings-"

"Doctor Cummings," She corrected him.

He took a moment to smirk before saying, "Doctor Cummings, you write an advice column for the local newspaper and you have a radio show and you were the editor for some big time magazine. It's not unusual to have some strange fans. Have you seen any unusual characters around your home? Has anyone been following you?"

"No. Nothing like that."

"Has he called you? Gone to your workplace? Or threatened you?"

"No…not a direct threat."

Officer Bishop handed the napkin back to Laci. "Until you have some evidence that actually shows someone is actually stalking you…I'm sorry but I can't help you." He turned away from her and began typing on his computer.

"Are you kidding me right now?" Laci was upset. "I'm telling you that I feel unsafe and you're telling me that's not good enough?"

Officer Bishop's face hardened as he looked at Laci. "Ma'am, you're telling me that someone is stalking you. I ask you for some proof. You tell me you got some weird e-mails and a napkin but none of them have a direct threat. You work in a position that puts you out in the public eye. From what I can tell…you don't have a stalker. You have a crackpot that wants attention. For now, my hands are tied. I cannot help you."

Laci wanted to scream but she silently counted to five before turning around and leaving Officer Bishop to his work.

"The Biggie Burger? Who had the Biggie Burger?"

"I did," two voices said in unison. Marie Ann Davis and a man she wished she knew spoke at the same time. They looked at one another and laughed.

"It's okay. You go ahead," the man told her with a smile. Marie Ann smiled back.

"I got two Biggie Burger!" the worker behind the counter shouted.

Both the man and Marie Ann stepped forward to claim their food.

"I wouldn't take you as the type to eat fast food. You look like you're really in shape," he told her.

Marie Ann couldn't help but smile despite thinking

his pickup line was horrible. "I have a weakness for burgers."

"Me too. I was hoping to get a quick bite to eat before I went to watch a movie," he said.

"With your girlfriend?" Marie Ann asked hoping it was subtle enough to find out if he had a girlfriend without seeming too interested.

"Actually, I was going to go by myself."

"Oh. Well going to a movie sounds like fun."

"Yeah well it would be more fun if I had a beautiful woman going with me."

Marie Ann laughed. He was cute. Too cute. Something must be wrong with him.

He cleared his throat, "I don't suppose you would like to go with me?"

Marie Ann smiled, "Well it depends."

"On what?"

"On what movie you wanted to see."

He smiled at her and answered, "I'll watch whatever you want to watch. My name is Judas by the way."

"Hi Judas. I'm Marie Ann."

"Marie Ann? That's a very unique name. I like it."

"Why thank you Judas."

The two ate their Biggie Burgers and then went to the movies where they watched some chick flick about an older woman falling in love with a younger man who turned out to be a serial killer. After the movie, the two of them went out for a walk at a local park.

"So Marie Ann, I see you keep fiddling with that ring you're wearing. Is it special to you? Are you secretly married?" He was laughing as he said it but Marie Ann stopped walking.

"How did you know?"

"You're married? I was just joking! Oh man…I'm sorry. I would-" Marie Ann's laughter stopped him from talking.

"Very funny," he shook his head.

"Sorry but of course I'm not married. I wouldn't have gone to the movies with you if I was."

Judas laughed at her admission. "I'm sorry. I once dated a married woman but I didn't know she was married."

"Are you serious? What happened?"

"Let's just say that her husband found out about it and it wasn't pretty."

Marie Ann laughed, "How horrible!"

"It was. So what's the deal with the ring?"

Marie Ann lifted the ring to be at eye level with her face, "It's beautiful isn't it? It was my grandmother's ring." It was white gold with a red ruby and opal stones surrounding it. Her friends had often told her how interesting and beautiful the ring was.

"It's beautiful," Judas admired.

The park they were at wasn't overly crowded. "Did you know that behind those trees, there's a pond with some ducks?"

Marie Ann shook her head, "No. I can't say I normally come to the park."

"Do you want to see it?"

Marie Ann couldn't help but be drawn into Judas's handsome face. "Sure. Why not?"

He grabbed her hand and dragged her behind the trees. Marie Ann was laughing until they were hidden from the other park-goers and frowned. "Ahh….there's no pond here."

She didn't get to see him lifting a rock and

slamming it into the back of her head. She was knocked out cold. He removed her ruby ring and lifted it to the moonlight. It really was beautiful and unique. He placed it in his pocket and pulled out a multipurpose knife that he carried. It would be difficult, but he knew he could use it to get the job done.

He leaned forward and whispered into Marie Ann's ear, "I'm sorry about this...but you really should have picked better friends."

"Laci is that you?"

"Andrew?"

"Yeah. Hey I'm sorry to bother you over the weekend but I just wanted to call and thank you again for the other night. You really helped me out of a bind."

"No problem."

"Okay...well I guess I'll see you tomorrow at work."

"Right. I'll see you tomorrow Andrew." Laci disconnected the call and turned around to see her brother Declan clucking his tongue at her.

"What?" she asked him.

"A guy calls you and you give him the cold shoulder. That's cruel sister."

"What are you talking about? He just called me to thank me."

"And you call yourself a psychologist. How can you ignore the signs that are right in front of you?"

"Declan...don't even go there. Dr. Brett is my

colleague and that's it."

"Riiight…and I'm Saint Declan."

"Whatever you want to call yourself is your business brother."

The sound of a really old Bobby Brown song filled the air.

"Is this the stone age? Change your ringtone!" Declan teased his sister.

"Oh shut up! It's my prerogative!" Declan started laughing and she answered the phone to a frantic Amber.

"Laci!"

"Amber what's the matter?"

"It's Marie Ann. Oh Laci!" Laci was having a hard time understanding her friend Amber. She would speak a few words and then break into tears.

"Okay Amber. I'm going to need you to take a deep breath."

"It's Marie Ann."

"What about Marie Ann?"

"She was mugged in the park."

"What? Oh my God. Is she okay?"

"Oh Laci. It's terrible."

"Amber! Get a hold of yourself. What happened to Marie Ann? Tell me slowly."

Laci could hear her friend sniffling on the other end of the line. "Her brother called me today from Florida. The police had contacted him because her ID was on her…but they took her money and her jewelry."

"They left her with her ID though?"

"Yeah it's like they wanted the police to know who she was."

"Well how is she? Is she at the hospital right now?"

"She's not at the hospital."

"Why not?"

"Because Laci…whoever did this…they didn't just mug her."

"What the heck Amber, how is Marie Ann?"

After a moment of silence, Amber finally answered, "She's dead."

CHAPTER 6

It was raining. Black umbrellas were circled around the plot of Marie Ann Davis with the exception of one pink and white polka-dotted umbrella.

Dr. Laci Cummings looked at her friend Amber who mouthed the words, "Sorry...I couldn't find a black umbrella."

Normally Laci would have smiled but today she felt numb. Her friend was dead. She had been brutally murdered and the police didn't know who had committed such a disturbing crime. She had been robbed. Marie Ann wasn't rich so her life was essentially valued at a few hundred dollars. Laci was devastated. She looked over at Jacob Davis, Marie Ann's brother. He was sobbing. Laci inhaled a shaky breath. Jacob was a Navy Seal. He was probably the bravest man she knew and here he was...sobbing over the death of his sister. Amber and Kay looked pale and distraught, mirroring how Laci assumed she looked as well. When the preacher finally said the last few words of his prayer, family members and friends began to step forward and place red roses over her casket.

He stood behind an old weather-beaten tree...watching. Dr. Cummings looked upset. He smiled. He could hear the thumping of the rain splattering against his umbrella but he couldn't remove himself from the scene. This was his doing. His actions brought Laci to this cemetery. If he wanted, he could bring her here again. Maybe next time it would be her funeral. He chuckled and turned around. As he walked back to his car, he couldn't help but whistle at how wonderful the day was.

"We're all going to Marie Ann's apartment. Does no one but me think that's weird?" Amber asked.

"It is weird," Kay chimed in from the backseat of Laci's Benz.

"Jacob isn't from here so it makes sense to have it at her place. Besides, it'll be therapeutic for us to see her things, look at her pictures, that sort of thing."

"Will you stop your psychobabble Laci and get real? No amount of picture book looking is going to make this better." Kay was sitting in the back seat with her arms crossed and her eyes closed.

"I know that...it's just that this may be good for us. We all miss her."

"I miss her like crazy," Amber whispered, "Who is going to get their nails done with me from now on?"

"Stop it Amber. I know what you're trying to do," Kay said with her eyes still closed.

"What am I trying to do?"

"Get one of us to go with you to the manicure place where they insult you in Korean. No thank you!"

Amber rolled her eyes, "One of our friends was just buried and all you can do is make jokes? Don't you care at all?"

Kay opened her eyes and grimaced, "Of course I care! Why wouldn't I care? Just because I'm not crying every five minutes doesn't mean I'm not sad."

Amber was about to snap back at Kay, so Laci intervened, "Okay you two that's enough. We're here."

They walked to Marie Ann's apartment and were instructed to leave their umbrellas, rain jackets, and purses in the spare bedroom.

As they were walking out of the room, Laci overheard Jacob, Marie Ann's brother, "I still can't believe it. All she had was our grandmother's ring and maybe less than a hundred dollars on her. Why would anyone want to kill her for that?"

Laci remembered the ring Jacob spoke about. Marie Ann always wore it and even once said that she would be buried in it. That wasn't able to happen. Someone else took that choice from her. As the gathering was coming to an end, Laci felt her phone vibrating. It was a text from her brother Declan.

"When are you coming home?"

She responded, "Within thirty minutes."

"Okay. See you later freckle face."

"Okay Beanie Meanie!" she texted back.

She gave a faint smile as she thought of Declan. She was lucky that he was still with her unlike Jacob and Marie Ann. She gave Jacob her condolences and grabbed her purse and jacket from the spare bedroom. Her friends were already waiting for her beside her car. Laci dropped them both off before heading home.

"Declan!" she shouted into the house. She walked into the living room, "Declan?"

The house was silent. "That's strange. He said he would be home," Laci whispered to herself. She was about to step into the kitchen when a hooded figure jumped in front of her.

Laci screamed and grabbed a decorative glass statue she had in the hallway. She screamed again and hit the hooded figure in the face.

"Dammit Laci! That hurt!"

Laci looked down to see her brother Declan, wearing a too tight Spiderman costume.

She giggled which turned into outright laughter, "What are you doing?"

"I was trying to cheer you up," Declan removed his hood and began rubbing his face.

"Declan you wore that costume when you were eighteen...how are you able to fit into it at twenty-four?"

"Duct tape and determination."

Laci looked at her brother, "What did you just say?"

"You don't want to know."

Laci began laughing as she thought of her huge brother fitting himself into a tight costume just to cheer her up. She smiled and hugged her brother, "Thank you Declan for being such a great brother. You really did cheer me up."

"That's not all. Dinner is on me sis," Declan began ushering Laci out the door.

"Declan, you're still in that costume!"

"So?"

Laci laughed in response, "You're going to go out in public like that? Where did you even find it?"

"In the attic. I started cleaning it out so I can use it

as a studio for my graphic designs." He put the hood back on and escorted Laci to his car.

"Sounds cool," Laci stifled a guffaw as the neighbors spotted her brother in his Spiderman costume. It was clearly too tight and he was walking very slowly so that he didn't rip the costume's cheap material.

"Where are we going?" Laci asked.

"The best place ever!"

Fifteen minutes later, they were waiting in the drive-thru of their local What-A-Burger, a fast food place.

"This is the best place ever?" Laci asked.

She laughed as Declan nodded in his Spiderman outfit. He pulled up to the drive thru and she continued to giggle as he ordered them two number fives all the way. She was in tears of laughter as he pulled up and the poor teenager that was working the window didn't know how to respond.

"That'll be twelve seventy-two sir," the pimpled teen mumbled.

"What? Superheroes don't eat for free?" Declan asked while Laci was looking out the passenger side window to stop herself from laughing.

"I could ask my manager," the teen said, clearly flustered.

"No need," Declan realized that he didn't have any pockets to put his wallet in.

"Typical!" Laci groaned, "Even Spiderman pulls this kind of trick to get out of paying." She handed him her debit card and he handed it to the cashier. On their way back home, Declan rolled down his window at a red intersection light. The young kids in the car next door to them kept banging their fists against the window to get his attention. Declan laughed and flicked them off. Laci gasped and hit her brother, who was driving, "Declan they're kids!"

"So?"

"So? You probably shattered their superhero dreams for life. What if they looked up to Spiderman?"

Declan shrugged, "They should learn early on in life that they have to look up to themselves not others."

"You're an idiot."

"Awww but sister, you have to love me anyway."

Laci was still laughing when they got home. Because of Declan, she had forgotten all about her grief from Marie Ann's passing...at least for the time being. As they came inside, Laci tossed her purse on the couch and followed her brother into the kitchen.

"I love you Declan."

"Eeew gross. We're just about to eat and you want to get all girly with me."

"Shut up. I'm serious. You're my brother and I love you so please...don't leave me like Marie Ann left Jacob. He looked so broken up at the funeral."

They were quiet for a moment, "Laci. You're my sister and I love to give you a hard time but if anything ever happened to you...I would be devastated. I mean...who else would financially support me?"

"Please, you probably make more money than me."

Declan grinned as he bit into his burger, "Yeah I probably do. I'm in high demand sister. High demand."

Laci rolled her eyes. "You weren't supposed to agree with me. I'm a famous psychologist. I make more money, remember?"

Declan shrugged.

"Anyway, don't forget...you can't die on me first."

Declan laughed, "I don't make promises I can't keep." He got up to get some paper towels but accidentally tugged too hard on the dispenser, causing the roll of towels to fall to the ground. He bent over to pick it up when they both heard a loud ripping sound followed by Declan cursing.

Laci pounded the table in laughter.

"Don't even say it Laci!" Declan wrapped paper towels around his waist and slowly walked to his bedroom to change out of his Spiderman costume.

He groaned in embarrassment as he heard his sister shout behind him, "You should have used more duct tape!"

She was running late and slammed her purse in between the closing elevator doors.

"So we meet here again," Dr. Andrew Brett smiled at her.

"Yeah. I guess we do."

"I'm sorry about your friend."

"Uhmm...thanks. I'm still wrapping my mind around the whole thing."

"I got your message about doing a show on losing your loved ones in a relationship. I think it'll be great."

"Thanks. I prepared a list of books that I thought I could share with our listeners."

"Sounds great," Andrew smiled at Laci and they

both walked to the office they were now sharing. Laci placed her purse on the desk she used and then left with Andrew to the sound booth.

"Where's your list of books?" Andrew asked about ten minutes after they had begun prepping for the show.

"Oh crap. I left it in my purse. Let me go get it. I'll be right back."

She sprinted to the office that they shared and bumped into a janitor who had a cap on and his face lowered as he was leaving her office, "Be careful miss."

"Oh sorry," she automatically responded, a little flustered to almost be run over by the giant waste bin he carted around.

She stepped into the office and a feeling of dread filled her. "What is up with me?" she asked herself. She spotted her purse sitting on her desk. A feeling of worry filled her, "You are a bad girl Laci Cummings," she said as she began checking her wallet to make sure her cards and money were still in place. She didn't know the janitor but she didn't want to take a chance that he may have gone through her purse that she left foolishly out in the open. Everything was in place. She rummaged through her purse for her list of books when something caught her eye.

She ran back outside of the room and down the hall but she didn't see the janitor.

"Laci? There you are! I've been looking for you. You need to hurry up and get back to the booth." George, her producer, was standing in the hallway, flagging her down.

"George, do you know where the janitor's office is at? I need to ask him a question."

"The janitor? I don't think they're here today. I think they only come in on the weekends. I don't know what cleaning issue you're having...but it can wait. Get back to the booth now!" George rushed back the way he came, leaving Laci alone in the hall while carrying her purse. She brought up her purse and pulled out the object that had caught her attention earlier. It was a ruby ring with small opals. She didn't know how it had been in her purse, but she knew, without a doubt...that it was her dead friend Marie Ann's ring.

CHAPTER 7

Officer Joe Bishop stared at Dr. Laci Cummings. She looked a bit shaken up but her story wasn't making sense.

"So tell me again...you found this ring inside your purse?" he asked.

Laci softly counted to five before answering, "Yes. For the tenth time...it was in my purse."

"And it may have belonged to your dead friend?"

His insensitive words caused her to scowl, "My friend that was recently murdered did own this ring. She wore it all the time."

"So how did it get in your purse?"

"How would I know?" Laci gave an exasperated groan. "Isn't it your job to figure that out?"

Officer Bishop smirked, "Okay Ms. Cummings-"

"Doctor Cummings," she corrected him again. She suspected he was addressing her incorrectly on purpose.

"Doctor Cummings. Do you know anyone that would have killed Marie Ann Davis and would also want to hurt you?"

"No. Not a soul."

"You said a man, a janitor, was coming out of your office. Did you get to see his face?"

"No. He was wearing a baseball cap and had his head down. He did have blonde hair though. I could see it coming out of his cap. George said the maintenance crew only comes in on the weekend so it seemed suspicious to see him."

Officer Bishop nodded, "Did you notice any tattoos on him? Like perhaps a bald eagle on his left forearm?"

"That's really specific. Ummm yeah. Now that I think of it, he did have a tattoo!"

"And he was wearing a gray uniform?"

"Yes!"

"Are you sure he only comes on the weekends?"

Laci gave a confused expression and followed the direction of Officer Bishop' expression. Talking to another worker, was a male janitor. He was smiling and laughing.

"I guess I'm not too sure."

"I'll talk to the janitor. Is there anything else you want to tell me?"

Laci clenched her fists, "I really think you should check the ring for fingerprints. I'm telling you that someone is stalking me and maybe that person killed Marie Ann. How else would that ring get into my purse?"

Officer Bishop pursed his lips together, "That's a very good question."

Laci could see the look of skepticism on his face and it angered her. Did he think she was some crazy woman? Dr. Andrew Brett, her cohost came towards them.

"Is everything okay?" he asked.

He looked from Laci to Officer Bishop. They seemed to be having some kind of staring contest.

"Everything is fine here Dr. Brett," Officer Bishop told Andrew.

Laci rolled her eyes at his ability to correctly address Andrew.

"Are you going to check the ring for fingerprints?"

"Yes. I will definitely be checking the ring for fingerprints."

She sighed in relief, "Good."

"Did you need anything else Officer?" Dr. Andrew asked.

"No, that'll be it for now. I'll go interview the janitor. Excuse me."

Laci cursed under her breath.

"What was that?" Andrew asked.

She shook her head, "Nothing. It's been a long day."

"Hey you were great. I can't believe you still did the show even though you were so shook up about the ring. Any other person wouldn't have been able to do that."

"I just thought that our topic tonight was important. Besides we also dedicated the show to Marie Ann tonight."

"How are you holding up?"

"I'm fine. I just need to get home."

Laci smiled as she left the building but something was bothering her. She had a nagging feeling that she couldn't shake. She felt like someone was watching her. She walked out into the parking lot and looked around. It had gotten late. The parking lot was void of any people. She scrambled inside her purse for her keys which she held in between her fingers. Years ago, her brother had taught her to hold the keys between her fingers, so if someone came up to try and attack her, she could punch them and the keys would cause extra damage that her strength didn't carry.

She could hear the traffic of the city surround her and one of the parking lot lights was flashing on and off. "This is like a scene from some scary movie," she whispered as she heard the snap of her heels against the pavement. She got closer to her car and noticed a gold envelope behind one of her windshield wipers.

She froze. She was a few steps away from her car and she looked around. Nothing. She could still hear the steady hum of the nearby traffic. She took a step forward...and then another. She reached an unsteady hand out to the small red envelope as her hand with the keys tightened.

Suddenly, the sound of an alarm blasted through the air. Laci realized that she had accidentally hit the panic button of her own car which caused the lights to flash and the alarm to sound off. She fumbled with her keys to get it to turn off. Two quick beeps and it was off. She sighed and laughed at herself. She quickly grabbed the red envelope.

"What do you think you're doing?"

Laci turned around to see an old man standing in front of her. She smiled. It was Eric, the security guard. He wasn't a very threatening figure but his job was to watch the parking lot.

"Hi Eric. It's me Dr. Cummings. I accidently set my own alarm off."

"What's that in your hand? A wedding invitation?"

"Uh...no. Not quite."

"Well hurry up and get home. It's not safe for a lady to be out in the dark by herself."

"I will. Thanks Eric."

He nodded and began to walk away, when a thought occurred to Laci. "Hey Eric. Did you see anyone leave this note on my car?"

"No. I can't say that I did."

She felt disappointment but smiled at him anyway, "Okay...I just thought I would ask."

"The security cameras might have caught it though."

"Really? Can we check?"

"Sure, let's go back to my office."

She followed the old security guard with the wobbly gait to his office.

He flipped on some mini television screens and frowned.

"What's wrong Eric?"

"My camera's gone out. I've been training the new guy so I haven't been watching the monitors in here. I'll have to report this."

Eric made some calls and grabbed a small toolkit. "I'm going to check on the camera. I'll be back. You stay here."

"It's okay...I should probably get going."

"No, just stay here. I'll be right back."

She didn't understand why Eric wanted her to wait for him. She sighed as she held the gold envelope in her hands.

"I guess I should open it."

She slowly tore open the envelope. Inside was a card of a lion stalking his prey in the wild. Scrawled inside the card was a message written especially for her.

"I'm still watching."

She dropped the card in fear and jumped when she saw a man standing in the doorway of Eric's office.

"Why are you so scared Dr. Cummings?"

Laci looked at Officer Bishop and despite her dislike for him, actually felt somewhat relieved.

"Thank God it's you. Someone left a note on my car." She bent down and quickly picked up the note. She handed it to him and he looked it over.

"Interesting," he said softly.

"What's interesting?"

"I came down here because security called a report to the station. Since I was already here, they asked me to check this out. Who knew this building would be such a hub of criminal activity?"

"I'm telling you that someone is trying to scare me. They're following me," Laci pointed to the note he was holding. "Doesn't that prove anything to you?"

He sighed and asked, "Listen Dr. Cummings. How long have you had to share a show with Dr. Andrew?"

"What? What does that have to do with anything?"

"Just answer the question."

"Less than two weeks. Not very long."

"Were you happy when you learned that you had to share a show?"

Laci didn't understand where this was going, "Not at first but I get along fine with Dr. Brett."

"Hmm…"

"What's that supposed to mean Officer Bishop? What are you getting at?"

"When did you say you received the first letter?"

"It was an e-mail. Dr. Brett read it on air. The man

basically said he was my stalker."

"Don't tell me you think Dr. Brett is behind all of this? He's a respected psychologist. He's written books. He'd be the last one to do something like this."

"So you don't think a psychologist can go a little crazy?" Officer Bishop asked her.

"No. That's not what I'm saying. It's actually not uncommon for a mental health professional to require counseling. We have to listen to all kinds of stressful stories. I just don't think it's Dr. Brett."

"I agree," Office Bishop nodded. "He has nothing to gain from this."

"You agree with me? So then who do you think could be doing this?"

"I don't think you are going to like my answer."

Laci fumed. She was getting very irritated with Officer Joe Bishop, "I'm pretty sure I can handle it. Who do you think is writing me these letters?"

Officer Bishop cocked his head to one side and answered her.

"You."

CHAPTER 8

Dr. Laci Cummings was fuming. She slammed the door as she came into her house, startling her brother, Declan, who was texting on his phone in the living room.

"Dang sis' who pissed you off?" he asked.

"Ugh I hate…I mean really hate him!"

Declan didn't know who she was talking about. "He sounds like a jerk. You want me to kick his ass?"

"Yes!"

Declan had been joking so he started laughing at her response, "Okay…tell me who he is first."

"Officer Joe Bishop."

"A cop? You're upset with a cop? What did he do? Give you a ticket for putting on make-up while driving again?"

"Ha ha," Laci laughed sarcastically. "That was one time when I was sixteen and no, he didn't give me a ticket."

"Then what did he do?"

"He basically accused me of being an attention

whore that sends herself stalker letters to get police attention." Laci sat down on the sofa next to her brother and crossed her arms.

"Wait. What?" Declan was trying to process everything his sister just told him. "Is someone sending you threatening letters?"

Laci sighed, "Yes."

"And the cops aren't doing anything about it?"

"Nope."

Declan stood up and grabbed his sister's hand, "C'mon, we're going to the police station right now."

Laci laughed at his desire to protect her, "Declan, it's okay. I'm fine. It just shocked me that an officer could be so callous to me."

"Maybe you got his girlfriend to dump him," Declan suggested.

"What are you talking about?"

"Oh c'mon Laci. Women eat up whatever crap you spew on your show. If you told women cops were horrible boyfriend material, I'm sure a few of your listeners would dump their police officer boyfriends."

"One, I would never do that. Two, I don't spew crap! Three, my listeners have minds of their own. They wouldn't dump someone just because I said so."

"Whatever, either way that officer shouldn't' be accusing you of doing something like that."

"No, he shouldn't. I took down his badge number to file a complaint on the narrow-minded pig."

Declan laughed.

"What's so funny?"

"You just called a cop a pig."

"Grow up Declan," Laci hit him with her purse as she passed him.

"Hey Laci," Declan called out as she mounted the

stairs, "Are you sure you don't want me to go with you to the police station? I don't like the fact that someone's sending you threatening letters."

Laci gave him a tremulous smile, "I'm okay Declan. It's probably just some weirdo playing a prank."

Declan crossed his arms, "If you need me. I'm here sis."

"Thanks brother…but you should get back to your text, your phone keeps dinging."

Declan smiled, "I get back in town and all the ladies are blowing my phone up."

She gave a half-hearted laugh and went to her room.

She flipped on her laptop and checked her e-mails from her advice column.

"Dear Laci,

My girlfriend recently cheated on me with a woman. She says it shouldn't bother me because it wasn't with a man and that she can't help the way she feels. She insists that she still loves me but I don't know if this is something I want in a relationship. —Confused Man"

Alex poised her hands above her keyboard and began typing,

"Dear Confused,

Being bisexual doesn't give you carte blanche to cheat with someone of the same gender. She's in a relationship with you and cheating is a betrayal of your trust. If you're not keen on an open relationship, I suggest you speak with your girlfriend and figure things out. This relationship will never succeed if you two aren't in agreement about what is and isn't acceptable in a relationship. Best of luck. —Laci"

Laci was about to look at the next e-mail when her phone dinged, notifying her of a message. It was from her producer, George.

"Don't forget you have to do a Q&A at the college tomorrow."

"Crap I forgot," she whispered to herself. Several weeks ago, she had agreed to hold a question and answer session for the students at Josephine Community College about building positive work relationships. Students would be allowed to ask questions and she would answer them from a professional standpoint. After everything that had happened, she really didn't feel like going.

"Do I even have anything to wear?" she asked herself. She yawned and got ready for bed, leaving her laptop on. She was too tired to think of anything else.

Kay stood at Marie Ann's grave.

"Hi Marie Ann," she softly spoke aloud. "I hope you're doing okay. I'm sure you're in…well wherever you believed you would be. I know you're probably surprised to see me. I'm the least emotional one out of our group. I just wanted to tell you that I miss you and I hope they catch whoever did this. I'm gonna keep bugging them until they do. Yeah…that's all for now. I'll see you in a few days, okay?"

Kay bent down and placed some lilies over her grave. She began to walk away when she noticed a man coming towards her with a gorgeous bouquet of white roses.

"Those are beautiful," she said to him without

thinking.

He stopped and looked down at the flowers, "They're for a friend of mine. We used to work together and I couldn't make it to her funeral."

"Really? That's too bad. I was here visiting my friend."

The man nodded and continued walking, Kay watched him as he stopped at Marie Ann's grave and placed the flowers down next to her lilies.

Kay didn't recognize the man. "Excuse me!" Kay raised her hand as she called out and he looked at her a bit surprised.

"I don't mean to disturb you, but I couldn't help but notice that you put flowers down next to Marie Ann's grave. You worked with her?"

The man nodded.

"She was my friend."

"Really? We used to work together years ago."

"Where?"

The man smiled, "I'd rather not admit it. It's too embarrassing."

Kay laughed.

He smiled at her and asked, "Would you like to get some coffee?"

Kay was taken aback. She was in a cemetery and this handsome man that had just put roses down on her friend's grave was asking her out to coffee. Kay wasn't sure if it was a bit too strange or if Marie Ann was sending her someone special to offer some consolation.

Kay nodded her head, "Sure. I'd love to. I'm Kay by the way."

He smiled back, "Nice to meet you Kay. I'm Judas."

Laci didn't know what to wear for her session with

the college kids. She was in her bedroom trying to choose between a red dress and a blue dress.

"I hate being a woman sometimes. We have the worst decisions," she joked to herself. She looked at the time on her laptop. She only had an hour to get there.

"Blue or Red? Make a decision Laci!" she told herself.

Suddenly her phone dinged. She looked at the message. It was from a number she didn't recognize.

"What time are you leaving?"

Laci was thrown off. She didn't recognize the number so it couldn't have been someone in her contacts list. She texted back, *"I'm sorry. Who is this?"*

"It's me dummy."

"Dummy?" now she was annoyed. *"I think you have the wrong number,"* she texted back.

"Oh. Sorry about that."

"No problem," she texted the anonymous offender.

She tried on the blue dress and the red dress, still unsure of what to wear. She looked at her laptop one more time. She only had thirty minutes but still couldn't decide. "I don't know which dress to wear!" she was exasperated and laid both dresses on the bed as she stood there in her slip and bra.

Her phone dinged again. She saw that it was the same wrong number from before. She read the message and gasped.

"I think you should wear the red dress."

CHAPTER 9

Fear pulsated through Laci as she stood by her bed and slowly looked around her room. When she didn't see anyone, she quickly grabbed the blue dress and threw it over herself. Having clothes on made her feel less vulnerable. Her windows were covered with thick curtains so she didn't understand how anyone could know that she was deciding what dress to wear.

"Is someone there?" she softly called out. "Hello?"

She looked down at her phone which was now quiet and typed a reply, *"Who is this?"*

She waited for a response.

Nothing.

She took a deep breath and began talking to herself, "Okay…think logically Laci. No one is in the room with you. No one can see you. There has to be a logical explanation."

Her mind reeled as she wondered how anyone could possibly have known what she was doing in her bedroom a few minutes before.

Declan!

Laci ran out of her room yelling, "Declan! If you think this is funny, you're sadly mistaken!"

She ran to his bedroom and opened the door.

He wasn't there.

She ran downstairs shouting his name. When she looked out the window and saw that his car wasn't in the driveway, her heart sank.

Declan wasn't home. She looked up to her bedroom and shivered.

"Maybe it was a coincidence," she told herself.

She grabbed a baseball bat that she kept in her coat closet downstairs and put her phone in her pocket. She slowly walked upstairs carrying the bat. She wasn't sure if someone was in the house with her so she didn't want to call the police yet.

"Hello," she called out again. She walked into her bedroom and quickly looked under the bed. She then dug the baseball bat into the curtains to make sure no one was hiding there either. She opened her closet and saw that it too was empty of any other person. She sat on her bed and looked at the text again to make sure she didn't just imagine it all. "I've got to get out of this house!" She grabbed her notes and purse and flew downstairs and out to her car.

Most of the students were seated and were waiting for her to arrive when she met the Joe at the entrance.

"So sorry I'm late."

"It's ok. They are so looking forward to hearing from you. I don't think they are minding at all."

Laci started walking down the corridor smoothing out the wrinkles she had acquired in her dress.
That's when her phone dinged again.

It was another message from her anonymous caller.
"You chose the blue. You look sexier in red. But you need you relax. Don't forget to smile; people love you but you have to remind them why."

"Oh my God," Laci tossed the phone away from

her as if it were possessed by something evil. Then she realized she didn't have a landline so she grabbed her phone again to call the police.

But first, she needed to call Andrew. She couldn't imagine herself dealing with a group of college students asking her about their relationship problems.

She quickly dialed Andrew, her colleague, who picked up after a few rings.

"Hey Laci. What's going on?"

"Andrew, I need a favor."

He laughed on the other line, "I'm fine, thanks for asking."

"I'm serious Andrew. I need you to cover for me tonight at the Q&A George mentioned the other day."

Andrew could hear the strain in her voice, "Are you okay Laci?"

"I'm fine," she whispered, "Can you do it?"

"Yeah sure. When is it again?"

"Tonight…like now, as in I was supposed to have started five minutes ago. I'm sorry for asking but I can't do it."

"Are you okay? You sound off. Like something's wrong."

"I said I'm fine."

"Don't forget I'm a psychologist too Laci. I can tell when someone's upset. What's going on?"

"I'll tell you later. Thanks for covering. I owe you big time. Call George if you have any questions.

Declan had arrived home a few minutes after Laci had called the police. He was standing by her now, with his arm around her shoulders as she explained to the police officers what had been happening to her the past few days.

One of the officers was taking notes and seemed empathetic while the other looked bored.

"Is something wrong Officer Bishop?" Laci asked him.

He shrugged his shoulders, "Nothing wrong with me. Please continue with my partner, Officer Stewart."

Laci could feel Declan' grip on her shoulder tighten. He was upset.

"It's okay Declan," Laci tried calming him.

Declan sneered at Officer Bishop.

"You have a problem with me?" Bishop asked Declan.

"And if I did?" Declan replied.

Officer Tracy Stewart cleared her throat, "Excuse me gentleman but we're in the middle of something here."

Neither man apologized; Tracy rolled her eyes.

"May I see your phone again Dr. Cummings?" Tracy asked. Laci handed her the phone and Tracy double-checked the phone number. "We'll track the number and see who it's registered to. That may help shed some light on what's going on."

"Thank you," Laci murmured.

Officer Stewart walked out of the living room leaving Officer Bishop behind. "I still have my theory on who's behind your stalking."

Laci stiffened and Declan gave a bitter laugh. "So this is the cop whose butt you want me to kick?"

"Declan!" Laci tried to get him to be quiet.

"You think you can kick my ass?" Bishop jeered.

"I don't think. I know. Don't act like you're tough because you have a badge. A tough guy wouldn't be picking on a defenseless woman."

"I seriously doubt your sister is defenseless."

Declan looked at Laci, "I told you. His girlfriend probably dumped him because of your show."

"Declan!" Laci wanted this to be over with.

"Shut the heck up!" Officer Bishop yelled.

Declan laughed, "Somebody better throw some mud down 'cause this pig needs to chill out."

"What the heck did you just say?"

"That's enough!" Laci shouted as she got in between both Declan and Officer Bishop. Officer Stewart walked back into the living room and assessed the scene, "Bishop let's go before you get into trouble."

Officer Bishop stared at Declan for a few beats before he turned around and followed Stewart.

"We'll let you know as soon as we find anything," the female officer told Laci.

"Thank you."

After they had left, Laci turned to her brother, "What the heck was that about Declan?"

"What? He was being a prick. I was just being one back."

Laci sat down with her phone still in her hands.

"Hey are you okay?"

Laci looked at her brother who was concerned. She shook her head. "I was scared Declan. I thought someone was hiding in that room…watching me."

"We already went through everything. No one was in there Laci."

"I know…but it's still scary."

Declan sat down next to his sister and hugged her. "You know…I'm here for you right?"

"Yeah I know. Remember? You promised not to die on me."

He laughed, "Yeah. I promise."

Officer Joe Bishop was throwing a stress ball up into the air, when his partner snatched it.

"What gives?" he asked her.

"What gives? I should be asking you that. You want to explain what happened at the psychologist's house?"

"Not really."

"C'mon Joe. Tell me what's up. It sounds like you two had a run in before."

"We did."

"That was very informative. You mind giving me an answer that's longer than two words?"

"Yes. I. Do. There, that's three words."

She playfully hit him on the head with the thin file that she was holding. "Butthole," she laughed.

Joe had smiled at her remark but as soon as she walked away, he frowned.

Dr. Laci Cummings.

He thought of what her brother had said while they were at her house.

"I told you. His girlfriend probably dumped him because of your show."

Declan Cummings wasn't completely off base. His girlfriend hadn't dumped him because of Dr.

Cummings's show. She had dumped him because of her friendship with Laci. Joe had thought Amber Griffin was his soulmate. She wasn't the perfect girlfriend but to Joe, she was very close.

He had put up with her constant comments on Laci' theories of a healthy relationship. He had told her many times not to take what Laci had said too seriously but Amber still listened to her friend. Joe remembered having to write up a dream journal because Amber heard Laci talking about the benefits of having one. At times he felt like there were three people in his relationship with Amber, and he had never even met Laci. He had avoided meeting the psychologist because he was convinced that she loved offering relationship advice to her friends. He thought that perhaps she adored the attention that came with being touted as a love expert. He didn't really think that Laci was sending herself notes and trying to get attention. He did think it was probably all harmless and she was just making the notes into a bigger deal than they needed to be.

He thought of how Amber had dumped him. It was when they were on the way to meet his parents. "Laci said that maybe I'm feeling anxious about our relationship because I'm not happy in it. I think she's right."

Joe had pleaded with Amber to give him another chance. She refused and continued to quote Dr. Cummings's advice on relationships.

"Hey what's wrong with you Bishop?"

Joe looked up to see his partner staring at him.

"I've been calling you but you were in some kind of daze."

"Sorry…what's up?"

She handed him a file, "The phone number that sent the texts to Dr. Cummings. Guess who it's registered to."

"Who?"

"Look at the file and see."

Joe opened the file and scanned the single sheet of paper that was in it. "You've got to be kidding me."

"Nope. Now what do you think is going on here?"

"I don't know, but I'm sure going to have fun finding out," he smirked.

He left the open file on his desk.

The name linked to the phone number was none other than Laci Cummings.

CHAPTER 10

Laci stood in her bedroom. The only light she had to see by was from the dim screen of her laptop. She could feel her body tense up as she slowly looked around and listened for any unusual noises. She had just done her nightly check of all the locks in the house. Every door and window leading to the outdoors was locked. As a single woman, even living in a fairly safe part of town, she knew there was no such thing as being overly cautious. Declan was living with her now, but she still felt a sense of comfort after making sure that everything was locked.

A cold draft from the small air conditioning vent blew over her, causing her to shiver. She quickly jumped into her bed and crawled under her sheets. She refused to turn on her bedroom light because that would be admitting defeat to the nameless person that was tormenting her. She didn't want to be afraid in her own home. No one should have that sort of power over her.

She was in her bed trying to fall asleep when the

door to her bedroom slowly opened, revealing a stream of light onto her face. "What the heck?"

"Are you asleep Laci?" Declan asked.

"Well I'm definitely not now," she muttered.

"Sorry. I just wanted to check on you."

"Just turn on the light Declan. I can't sleep anyway."

He flipped the switch, causing the room to be flooded in light. "Stop trying to be braver than you are and admit that you're scared shitless right now."

Laci frowned, "Did you seriously come here just to tell me that?"

"I know you Laci. You try to act tough and independent...but you're not fooling me. This is exactly like the time when mom and dad died."

Laci didn't respond so he continued, "You tried to act like you were okay but I saw you Laci. Crying in the kitchen...I saw you."

"So what? Our parents just died. Of course I'm going to cry! Is there something wrong with that?"

"Chill sis. No need to be so defensive. There's nothing wrong with it. I'm just saying that in front of me you were trying to be this brave and strong person...but you didn't need to be."

Laci hadn't realized that her eyes were watering. She stifled back a sob and wiped her eyes, "You're younger than me. I didn't want you to be more scared than you already were. It was just you and me. We're all we have left in this family."

Declan chuckled, "Laci I was twenty-one. Stop acting like I'm a kid. If you're scared...tell me. I can help you just like you would help me."

"And how can you help me? Somebody was watching me Declan but I have no idea how. Heck, for all I know they could be watching me right now!" The thought sent a ripple of fear through her body and she hid her face in her hands.

"Well…you can talk to me. Also, there's this…" he had been holding a red gift bag and he placed it in front of her, "Ta daaaa! Your baby brother is bearing gifts."

Laci sniffled and wiped her eyes again. She looked at the red bag and back to Declan, "What is it?"

"Open it and see," he urged.

She opened the bag and sighed, "You're an idiot Declan." She pulled out a DVD of The Karate Kid.

He started laughing, "What? Everything you need to know about fighting is in that film Laci!"

Also in the bag were a pair of brass knuckles, some pepper spray, and a Taser.

Laci was shocked. "Where did you get all this? Is it even legal to have?"

Declan shrugged, "I know people."

"Apparently we need to talk about your association."

"Hey, they're not bad…their behaviors are bad. Isn't that what all you shrinks say?"

Laci rolled her eyes. "Thanks Declan." Despite the fact that she wouldn't carry around so many weapons in her purse, he had once again cheered her up.

"You're my sister. Of course I'm going to help you out."

Laci gave a weak smile as she put everything back into the bag.

"Laci, the police will catch this guy."

She nodded, "As long as that Bishop cop isn't in charge of things, I'm sure they will. God, did you see the way he looked at me Declan? Like I was pond scum? He practically accused me of lying. Why would

I make any of this up?"

"He's a joke. Just forget about him. Besides, his partner seemed like she knew what she was doing and she was pretty cute."

"Will you stop? I'm trying to be serious here Declan."

"So am I! She was cute. Maybe I'll ask her for her number."

"That's my brother folks…the perpetual horn dog."

"Don't you mean corn dog?"

Laci laughed, "No! Are you sure you graduated college?"

Declan laughed, "See? You're not scared anymore are you?"

She shook her head, "No. Thank you Declan. If you want, I can set you up with one of my friends."

"No way!"

"What? Why wouldn't you want to date one of my friends?"

"I can only imagine how horrible it would be. My sister, the love doctor, giving advice to her friend who happens to be my girlfriend? Heck no! That wouldn't work."

"Okay fine. I won't set you up. Try and get a girlfriend all on your own."

Declan laughed, "How did we start talking about my love life?"

"I'm not sure but you should go to bed. I'll be fine. I have to see clients tomorrow morning so I need to rest."

"More wackadoos coming to the house," Declan whispered as he got up and left Laci to herself. She felt better knowing that her brother was there for her.

She wasn't sure if she could handle this alone. She hoped that Officer Stewart was able to discover who was sending her texts.

"Laci I'm meeting my friend Daniel. We're gonna grab some lunch at Jalisco's. You wanna come with us?"

Laci was busy looking through some files in her study, "No. I have to see a couple, remember? They'll be here any minute so make yourself scarce. Eat an enchilada for me."

Declan smiled, "I'll eat a whole plate of them for you!"

"Just don't come crying to me when you have bubble guts!"

Declan scrunched his face in mock horror, "Do your clients know how nasty you are sometimes?"

"Do your girlfriends know how nasty you are?"

He winked, "If they're lucky."

She laughed and threw a stress ball at him, "Get out of here!"

He quickly left before she threw something else at him. Ten minutes later the doorbell rang. Laci opened the door to see one of her more entertaining couples. Carrie and Phillip Baker. Phillip was a total conspiracy theorist which drove Carrie nuts. When they had first started dating, she thought it was a small quirk but his theories began to evolve and escalate over the years. What she once thought was adorable was now annoying.

"Hi Mr. and Mrs. Baker. Follow me," Laci led them

to her study.

Phillip Baker was looking around the office. "There aren't any secret listening devices in here are there?"

His wife Carrie rolled her eyes.

"No, there aren't any secret listening devices in here," Laci smiled at him.

It was a long session for Laci. She tried to help Carrie and Phillip come up with a compromise of having a set time to discuss his many theories with Carrie. In turn, Carrie suggested Phillip spend time with her exercising to some workout on their Xbox Kinect.

"No! I hate the Kinect Carrie. It's just another way for the government to spy on us," Phillip crossed his arms as he sat on the leather couch in Laci' office.

"If you expect me to listen to you rant about how the president is really an alien…then you should do a simple workout with me on the Xbox," Carrie also crossed her arms.

"Carrie, I'm serious. Nowadays people can easily spy on you through your Kinect, your laptop, even your cellphone. Don't you watch Dateline?"

"Is that show still even on?" Carrie asked.

Normally, Laci would've stopped Phillip from going on about one of his conspiracy theories but this was interesting to her. "What do you mean? How is that possible?"

Seeing that he had a willing ear, Phillip leaned forward and smiled. "You believe me, don't you? Well…it's easy. It takes less than five minutes for anyone to hack into your system."

"How do they do that?" Laci asked before she could stop herself.

"Dr. Cummings!" Carrie couldn't believe Laci was

practically egging him on to continue.

"That's easy. They do it through your e-mail."

"E-mail?"

"Yes. A complex bit of code delivered to you via a simple e-mail. You open up their Trojan horse and bam! They're spying on you. I heard of a case where a man was spying on several hundred women. He even started blackmailing some of them. You can google that. It's true."

"Blackmailing them?"

"Yeah. I mean…we do all sorts of things in front of an open laptop. Shoot, I bet most people carry around their phones with them everywhere they go. I bet you'd think twice if you knew someone was looking at you from the camera of it."

Laci didn't realize that she was leaning forward in her chair, she was so fascinated with what Phillip Baker was telling her.

"How would you know if someone sent you one of these e-mails?"

"You don't. Not unless they try to blackmail you…or you get your computer checked out." Phillip held up his smart phone. Laci noticed that the front and back camera on his phone were covered with black electrical tape. "You see that? Right now my phone is off, because I don't want them to listen in. When I turn my phone back on, they might be able to hear me but they won't be able to see me."

Carrie sighed, "He did the same thing to our laptops at home. I have to remove the tape anytime I want to skype."

"So any kind of e-mail can carry this…Trojan horse?"

"It's usually with some sort of attachment. Have

you opened any e-mails with attachments?"

Laci thought back and couldn't remember downloading any odd attachments. She saw Carrie who was looking at her watch and remembered she needed to remain professional. This wasn't the time to be exploring possible stalkers. She navigated the conversation away from Phillip's theory of people watching him through his phone's camera and eventually ended the session. As soon as they were gone, she ran upstairs to her laptop.

She stared at it as it sat open. It was always open. "This has to be it. There's no other explanation," Laci sat down in front of it and began combing through her personal e-mails. All of them were from people she knew and trusted. Then it hit her.

The advice column e-mails.

She had only received one e-mail. "Duh Laci. How could you forget?"

She was talking to herself as she scrolled to the e-mail that was an e-card. She had to download the attachment to see it and for it to play the music. She placed a small post it in front of the computer's webcam. She then dialed the police and asked to speak with Officer Stewart.

"Yes, Dr. Cummings. I'll be sure to note that in our file. You're going to have it checked out? That's a good idea. Be sure to let me know what they find ma'am."

Officer Stewart looked at her partner Joe Bishop who was smirking at her.

"What?" she asked him in a defensive tone.

"Why didn't you just tell her that you know she's full of it?"

"Will you stop being an ass for once and do your

job? What if someone is really stalking her? There are a lot of ways for someone to get a phone in another person's name. It's not totally unheard of you know."

"Yeah…yeah."

Officer Stewart didn't understand why her partner was giving Dr. Cummings such a hard time. He wasn't always such a jerk…well not to the extent that he was to Laci Cummings.

"Yeah well unless you want another complaint from her, maybe you should just keep your personal feelings to yourself."

"Personal feelings?"

"Did I stutter? I've worked with you for a few years and although you always have a bad attitude it's not usually this bad. The only thing I can figure is that you have a personal reason for not liking her."

Officer Bishop laughed. He genuinely liked his partner Tracy Stewart. She was blunt and didn't beat around the bush. She was also a good officer. "Will you stop treating me like a case? Fine! I promise not to get upset over the fact that Dr. Cummings is probably leading us on a wild goose chase."

"I don't know. She seems to have a lot of strange things happening to her."

Bishop sighed, "Let's just focus on something else right now. We have tons of other cases to deal with besides Dr. Cummings's."

Officer Stewart looked at her partner with an inquisitive face. There was something personal about his dislike for Dr. Cummings and she was going to find out why.

"So we're going to Best Buy…because why exactly?" Declan asked his sister Laci.

"Because I think someone sent me a virus and I want their Geek squad to look at it."

Declan and Laci dropped the laptop off and Declan told Laci that he still wanted to look around the store. While Declan went to look for some headphones, she found herself in the camcorder section.

She saw herself on the big television screens as she stood in front of the camcorder that the store televisions were connected to. The more she thought of someone watching her, the more disturbed she became. What else had she done in front of her camera? She changed clothes, walked around in her underwear, burped, and probably a few other million things she wouldn't want anyone else to see her doing.

"Is there anything I can help you find?" one of the workers asked.

"No thanks. I was just looking."

Just then her phone began to ring. It was an anonymous number. Laci didn't usually pick up anonymous numbers but today she did.

"Hello?"

She heard static on the other end…and heavy breathing.

"Hello, who is this?" she asked. When no one responded, she said, "If you don't answer who you are, I'm going to hang up."

"You covered my window…but I'll still be watching."

"Who the heck are you?"

"If you go to the cops again…I won't just be

watching anymore."

"What are you talking about?"

"You heard me."

"Hello? Hello?" Laci looked at her phone. The call had been disconnected.

"Ma'am are you okay?"

Still in shock, Laci looked up, "I'm fine. Thanks." He gave her an odd look and walked away.

Then her phone dinged. It was a message. Laci looked at the phone number. It was from the same number that she had received the texts from the day before. It was a picture of her friend Kay in a coffee shop. It was taken from a distance and she was sitting alone and smiling into her mug of coffee.

"What the heck?" Laci whispered.

Another ding from her phone notified her of a second message. She read it and her knees almost buckled.

"Stay away from the cops. You wouldn't want another dead friend, would you?"

Laci gasped, fear penetrating every fiber of her being. She looked up and could see her face again in the large TVs connected to the camcorder she was standing in front of. The look of horror was shocking and Laci couldn't help but see the irony. This is exactly what her stalker wanted…her fear on display.

CHAPTER 11

Officer Joe Bishop looked at his partner Tracy Stewart who was putting her phone back on its receiver.

"What was that about?" he asked.

Tracy looked at him in disbelief, "You're never going to guess."

"I don't want to guess. That's why I asked you," Joe smirked.

Tracy rolled her eyes, "That was Dr. Laci Cummings. She said she wanted to drop her complaint about someone following her."

Joe, who had been leaning back against his chair, suddenly sat up, "What?"

"Surprising right? She was so adamant the other day," Tracy began tapping her desk with her fingernails as she tried to figure out the reasoning behind it.

"We should charger her for wasting our time," Joe muttered.

"It makes no sense."

"What makes no sense?"

"Dr. Cummings. She was so shook up the other day. Even now she sounded frightened so why would she drop her complaint?"

"C'mon Tracy. We were going to tell her about the phone number being in her name. She probably wanted to back out of this attention seeking problem before she realized we were on to her sick games."

"And what about the ring? Marie Ann Davis's brother confirmed that was his sister's ring," Tracy reminded Joe.

"There were no prints on it. It's possible that Marie Ann had lent it to Dr. Cummings before she died."

"Women don't lend out precious family heirlooms Joe. At least I wouldn't. No, something isn't right here."

Joe leaned forward, "Are you thinking Dr. Cummings killed Marie Ann?"

Tracy scowled at her partner, "Would you mind being a professional and stopping your 'I hate Laci Cummings game' for a minute? I'm serious. It had crossed my mind for a minute but she wouldn't have the strength to do that to her friend. I spoke with the ME and based on the wounds, it had to have been someone taller and stronger than Marie Ann. Marie Ann was taller than Laci."

Joe shrugged, "Anything's possible when you're upset enough."

"People don't grow a foot and then shrink. No, something isn't adding up here."

Joe nodded, "Just admit it Stewart. You're thinking Dr. Cummings is suspicious too."

"No. Unlike you, I don't hate her. I'm thinking maybe she really is being harassed."

"Tracy, the phone was in her name!"

"Yeah but it was a pay-as-you-go account. Anyone could go to their local Wal-Mart and buy a phone card that most networks sell and set it up with a used phone and a Visa gift card online. I could even set up an account in your name if I wanted to."

"That's a bit of a stretch. It's easier to go with the theory that she's doing all of this herself and only wants attention."

"Since when did we just follow the easy route?"

"Since it's usually the right route," Joe retorted.

Tracy sighed, "I'm not going to drop this just yet. I could've sworn that she still sounded scared over the phone."

☐

CHAPTER 12

Laci walked to the parking lot.

"Just my luck," she muttered at the lack of people. She wondered if Eric, the security guard, was around. She clutched her pepper spray, still hidden inside her purse. She slowly walked forward, her red heels tapping against the hard cement. She was nervous and on edge.

A hand on her shoulder startled her. She screamed and turned around, quickly raising the pepper spray and hitting the nozzle.

"Arrghh! Dangit what the heck are you doing?"

Laci was still screaming even after she lowered the pepper spray. She watched in horror as the man continued to groan in pain in front of her. She knew him and this wasn't going to be a pleasant confrontation.

"I'm coming!" an old man's voice shouted. Laci looked up to see Eric, the security guard, scrambling towards them. "Dr. Cummings are you okay? Was this man trying to attack you?"

Laci didn't know what to say. Part of her was shocked by what she had just done and another part of her wanted to laugh at the ridiculous situation she was in.

"Heck no I wasn't trying to attack her! I'm a cop you old geezer!" the man shouted as he continued to stay in a doubled over position.

"Who're you calling old?" Eric asked as he touched the small gun he had at his waist.

"Sorry Eric, I thought he was trying to attack me...but he wasn't. It was just a misunderstanding."

Officer Joe Bishop straightened himself and sneered at Laci. His eyes were red from the pepper spray, "Misunderstanding? Is that what you call this?" he asked pointing to his red eyes.

"Well you came up from behind and scared me!"

"I'm a police officer!"

Laci ignored that comment, "How was I supposed to know that? Why did you call me down here? To accuse me of lying again?"

"I needed to talk to you."

"So you know this man?" Eric interrupted.

"Yeah she does...so go back to being a rent-a-cop," Joe didn't want an audience to the conversation he was about to have with Laci.

"Don't talk to him that way!" Laci couldn't believe that Officer Bishop could be so rude to everyone he came into contact with.

"Don't worry Dr. Cummings. Young punks like him don't bother me. Are you sure you're okay being alone with him?" Eric asked.

Laci nodded, "I'll be fine Eric. Thank you."

"Not a problem." The old security guard turned to look at Joe, "I'll be watching you through the cameras." Before Joe could respond, Eric began walking back to his security booth.

"What was that about?" Laci asked, "Why were you so rude to him?"

Joe shrugged, "Does it matter? Listen, we need to talk."

"Actually, we don't," Laci began to walk away when Joe grabbed her arm. "Let me go."

"I want to know why you dropped your complaint."

"That's it? You came all the way over here to ask me why I stopped reporting that I was being stalked? Didn't you accuse me of lying?"

"Look…I'm only asking because my partner made me feel guilty. She said I was being a jerk and no woman would feel comfortable making a report to me if I treated them the way I treated you."

Laci shook her head, "You're unbelievable. Is this your way of apologizing?"

"Well what do you expect? You say someone is stalking you and sending you strange messages. Imagine our surprise when we find out the number is registered to you!"

"What did you say?"

"Don't make me repeat myself, Laci. You know the phone number is registered to you."

Laci stared at Officer Bishop, "No it's not."

"You can stop pretending now. I know that's why you dropped the complaint. Stewart already said she's not going to pursue it but wasting police time isn't exactly okay."

Laci didn't understand how anyone could register her name for a phone line, "How is that possible? I mean how could someone use my name to get a phone?"

He gave her a suspicious look but answered, "That's easy. They just need your social security number and a date of birth. That information is getting easier to find."

"My social security number and date of birth?"

"If you're saying it's not your phone then that would mean someone opened a phone in your name. Aren't you going to ask me to look into it? Don't you want me to find out who used your name?"

"No!" She answered a bit forcefully and much too quickly for Officer Bishop not to be suspicious.

"What's going on? If you didn't open the phone someone did it in your name. That means they have your social and date of birth. You don't care?"

"What does it matter to you? I'm just a liar that wants attention, isn't that right?"

"Look that isn't the only reason I came by to see you. I've been thinking about why I've been too hard on you."

Laci didn't bother to respond. She was still thinking about the fact that her stalker had her personal information. She was making a mental note to call the credit bureaus. She wished Officer Bishop would stop talking to her. He wasn't her favorite person in the world and she just wanted to get home. She wasn't really paying attention to what he was saying until he began waving his hands in front of her face. She took a step back and swatted his hands away, "What are you doing? Stop that."

"Are you even listening to what I'm saying?" he asked.

She wanted to scream, "No, I could care less about what you have to say!" Instead she counted to five in her head and asked, "What were you saying?"

Joe ran his hands through his hair and repeated himself, "I said I need your help. Please."

Now she wished she had been paying attention. She didn't miss the irony of the situation. He needed her help. He even said the word please. She couldn't help but give a bitter laugh, "Why should I help you? When I asked you for help...you accused me of being a liar."

"Look I know we didn't start off on the right foot, but I've been thinking about things."

"Yes?"

"Even though I still don't believe that you have a stalker...I shouldn't have been so rude to you."

Laci chose to ignore his veiled accusation that she was liar and cocked her head to one side, "Who are you and what have you done with the real Officer Bishop? Are you actually admitting you were rude and that you made a mistake?"

Joe sighed, "I deserve that. Look...forget it. This was a stupid idea anyway."

Laci watched him start to walk away. "Wait." She had a resigned tone in her voice which meant she was probably going to regret helping him, "What did you need help with?"

"Last night I was up thinking about you."

Laci took a step back.

"Not in a creepy sort of way," Joe explained, "I was thinking about why I disliked you so much."

"Are you going to get to the point anytime soon? Because you're really making me regret hearing you out."

"Listen, you're friends with my ex-girlfriend."

Laci didn't believe him. None of her friends would

date such a jerk. "I'm sorry but I don't remember any of my friends dating you."

"It wasn't that long just a few weeks but I really thought I loved her."

Laci was still confused, "Why are you telling me this?"

"I want you to help me get her back."

"I'm sorry…say that again."

"Help me get my girlfriend back."

"Why would I do that? You're not exactly a nice guy Officer Bishop."

"I'm only like that with you… well, and my brother…and now Eric."

"Okay fine! I'm not a nice guy but that doesn't mean I don't deserve a second chance. I thought you shrinks were supposed to believe in helping people."

"That's interesting. I thought the same thing about police officers." Her sarcasm wasn't lost on Joe. "Listen, I'm not sure which of my friends you dated and quite frankly, I don't want to know. I try not to get involved in their love lives unless they really need my help."

"Don't lie. Amber used to quote you all the time."

"Amber? You dated Amber? Why am I not surprised? I don't give her relationship advice. She tends to latch on to whatever I say during the radio show and runs with it. I'm not sure what she told you but you should talk to her if you want to get back together."

"So you're not going to help me?"

Laci shook her head, "No. I'm sorry but I don't want to get involved. This is between you and her."

Joe closed his eyes, still feeling the sting from the pepper spray. Laci was eager to get away from him and as she approached her car, she noticed another gold envelope tucked beneath a windshield wiper.

She looked around before pulling it out and opening it. A small message was scrawled on a plain white card.

"Don't forget. No cops."

Laci texted her friend Kay, "Let's meet tomorrow."

She got into her car and drove home only to see a stranger's car in her driveway. She walked inside with apprehension which quickly turned into anger. Inside her living room was Declan with three of his friends watching a basketball game. They were drinking and eating McDonald's.

"Declan can we talk in the kitchen, please?"

Declan could tell his sister was upset, "Hey guys, this is my sister Laci." Laci was greeted with words, whistles, and catcalls.

"Idiots," she muttered as she walked to the kitchen with Declan in tow.

"Before you get really pissed, I have a good reason for inviting the guys over."

"It better be one heck of a good reason."

"The Hawks are playing."

Laci rolled her eyes, "You invited some friends over to watch a basketball game when you know what I've been dealing with? Couldn't you have just gone to a sports bar?"

"I'm sorry Laci but Robert called and you know we've been friends forever. He and his girlfriend just broke up and he didn't want to be at a bar."

Laci couldn't imagine any of the drunk guys in the living room as heartbroken, "I don't know them Declan. What if they're the ones stalking me?"

Declan began laughing, "Trust me they aren't

stalking you."

"What's that supposed to mean?" she was irked at the way he said the word you.

"Nothing it's just that you're old."

"Old!"

"Sorry…older. If you're over twenty-five they won't be interested. Besides you're my sister. They wouldn't mess with you."

"You never know what people do behind closed doors Declan. It's not good to make assumptions."

"Fine. I'll make sure they leave after the game. It's almost over anyway."

"They've been drinking."

"Robert's not drunk. He just always acts that way. He's been drinking soda all night."

"Fine." Laci left Declan in the kitchen to go upstairs and take a shower. The day had been strange and stressful for her. She let the cool spray of the water wash over her and when she was done, she wrapped herself in a large fluffy towel. She walked into her bedroom and began looking for some pajamas.

"Laci?"

"What do you want Declan?"

"Laci?"

"What do you want? Say what you want and get out. I have to change." Laci hadn't bothered to turn around as she rummaged through her drawers for a pajama set.

"Laci."

"What?" she yelled as she turned around expecting to see her brother. She was alone. She looked around and the hair on her neck stood up. "Declan?" She took a few hesitant steps forward, "Hello?"

When no one responded, she ran to the bathroom and quickly put on her clothes. She slowly opened her bathroom door which was connected to the master bedroom, and peeked out. She still didn't see anyone. She stepped outside and looked around again. She didn't hear anything.

"Did I imagine it?"

She walked out of her room and downstairs. Declan and his friends were gone. The sound of the front door opening, startled her and she let out a loud yelp.

"Laci? What's wrong with you?" Declan asked as he closed the door behind him.

"Where were you?"

"I followed the guys home to make sure they got to Robert's safely. They're all going to crash there for the night. I just got back. Is something wrong? You look weird."

Laci wondered if she should tell Declan. She opted not to, thinking it was just her imagination. "I'm fine. It's getting late. I'm going to bed."

"Okay. Nite." Declan sat back on the sofa and continued to watch the sports channel.

"Nite." Laci went back to her bedroom and walked inside. She didn't hear anything. She was about to pull back her covers when it called out again in a whispering voice.

"Laci."

Laci screamed and called out for Declan, who came running up the stairs, "What's wrong Laci?"

"I think there's someone in the room. I keep hearing someone whispering my name. Declan gave her a strange look but proceeded to look around her room.

"Laci, I don't see anyone. Are you sure you heard

something?"

She nodded.

Declan cleared his throat, "Is it possible you thought you heard someone? You've been under a lot of stress lately."

Laci wasn't sure anymore. She could've sworn she had heard someone. Maybe Declan was right. "Yeah you're right Declan. I'm just exhausted. I probably just need some sleep."

Declan stared at her for a moment, "Are you sure you're okay?"

"I'm fine. Go finish watching your show. I'm going to bed."

"Well I'll be right downstairs," he said as he walked out of her room, "Just holler if you need me."

"I will thanks."

Laci crawled under her sheets and closed her eyes. She wanted to sleep but the whispering voice returned.

"Sweet dreams Laci."

If she had been asleep, the piercing scream from her throat would've woken her.

CHAPTER 13

"Laci are you okay? What's going on?"

The light was switched on to reveal Laci holding on to her comforter in the middle of the bed. Declan saw the wild look of fear in his sister's eyes. "Laci," he said cautiously.

"He's here Declan. I heard him," Laci whispered.

"Who's here?"

"My stalker," Laci looked as if she was going to scream again.

"Did you see him?" Declan began whispering as well.

Laci shook her head, "I heard him."

"Okay…I'm going to look around." Declan proceeded to check under her bed and through the closet and adjoining bathroom. He didn't see anyone. He even checked the window to make sure it was locked. "Laci. No one is here. Are you sure you heard someone?"

"Yes, I'm sure!"

Laci watched the look of confusion on her brother's

face turn into concern.

"I'm not crazy Declan! I swear I heard someone."

Declan nodded, "Well I didn't find anyone here so what do you want to do? Should we call the cops?" Declan glanced at Laci' cell phone which was charging on her nightstand.

"And tell them what? That I'm hearing someone whisper to me in the dark? I'll sound like a lunatic."

"Then what do you want to do?"

"I don't know." Laci began biting her thumbnail…a nervous habit she hadn't engaged in since she was a teenager.

Declan walked over to Laci and grabbed her pillow and comforter, "Follow me."

"What are you doing?"

"Just follow me." Declan walked downstairs and tossed her blanket and pillow on the floor.

"Declan!"

He then went to his room and grabbed his blanket and pillow. "We're going to do something we haven't done in years Laci."

"What's that?"

"A living room campout!"

"Declan, we're too old to be sleeping on the floor."

"Speak for yourself woman!" Declan tossed their blankets on the floor along with their pillows. The house was dark except for the glow from the television in the living room. "Listen Laci…I know you've been stressed out lately. I didn't see anyone upstairs so let's just sleep downstairs for tonight until we can figure out what you heard in your bedroom. Maybe it was just some random noise that you think sounded like someone whispering to you like the AC vents turning on."

"It wasn't an AC vent but fine…just for tonight Declan."

Declan laughed, "Hey Laci…do you want to tell ghost stories?"

Laci didn't respond. Instead she tossed a pillow from the sofa at him.

"I'll take that as a no," Declan whispered.

The two of them settled in on the floor and slept. Laci was grateful that Declan wasn't directly calling her crazy or a coward. She felt like both.

A few hours later, Laci woke up and sighed. She wasn't getting much sleep because the floor was too uncomfortable. She thought about sleeping on the sofa but it would also be uncomfortable. She thought about what Declan had said earlier and wondered if her mind wasn't playing tricks on her. As a psychologist, she understood more than most how stress could affect a person's mind. It was totally plausible that it was all in her head. She hated being afraid in her own home and she resented the man that had sent her the notes and texts in order to scare her.

Laci sat up and looked over at her brother Declan. He was fast asleep with his arms spread out. Laci smiled. Declan was a good brother. He even sacrificed his bed so she wouldn't be afraid tonight. She got up and tiptoed to the staircase. Laci didn't want to be afraid to sleep in her own bedroom. She walked up slowly in the dark. When she got to her room, she ran to her bathroom and turned on the light switch. She then walked to her bed and laid down.

For her, this was a test in bravery. Eventually she drifted into a fitful sleep. An hour later, she awoke. Her eyes adjusted to the darkness and she could see a figure standing in her bedroom doorway.

"Declan?" she whispered.

The figure didn't speak. She couldn't see any distinguishable features, just the outline of his body as he stood in the doorway.

"Declan what are you doing?" she asked. The bathroom light wasn't enough for her to see by but it did allow her to catch a glimpse of the knife he held in his arm. "Declan?"

The man still didn't answer. Laci was frozen with fear. "Declan!" Laci screamed, hoping to wake her brother up. The dreadful thought that Declan could be dead downstairs filled her mind. She screamed again and the figure at her doorway ran away.

"Crap! Laci stay in your room! Call 911! Now!"

Laci gave a quick prayer of thanks as she heard her brother yelling from downstairs. She quickly grabbed her cellphone and dialed the police. She heard her brother groaning, glass breaking, and then a loud thud.

"Declan?" Laci had quickly given her house information to the 911 dispatcher and had ignored her instructions to stay on the line. She disconnected the call and walked to the edge of the staircase. She could see the front door open and Declan on the floor.

"Declan!" Laci ran towards her brother who wasn't moving. She got on the floor and began calling his name. She noticed the bruise on his face and a deep scratch on his left upper arm. "Oh my God. Declan wake up!" She lightly patted his cheeks until he emitted a soft groan.

"Declan wake up,"

"Enough already," he moaned. "What the heck

happened?"

"Are you okay?" Laci asked.

"Where is he?" Declan asked.

"I don't know. I think he ran out," Laci said as she looked at the open front door.

A few minutes later the police and an ambulance arrived to find Laci and Declan sitting on the sofa. Declan had a bag of mixed veggies over his eye. The paramedics bandaged up the cut on his arm.

"This is a fairly nice neighborhood," the officer remarked, "And you said you didn't notice anything missing?"

Laci shook her head, "I don't know. We haven't really checked but all of the valuables are in a safe. He was just watching me while I slept I guess…"

"And you didn't see his face?" the officer asked looking at Declan who cursed under his breath.

"No, he had some kind of ski mask on. He was dressed in black. That's all I remember before he hit me over the head with a vase."

The officer nodded and finished taking their statements.

After they left Declan looked at Laci, "I don't know what's going on but we need to get a security system installed."

Laci nodded. Tonight was scary. Laci wondered if the intruder had been hiding in the house or had he picked the lock and broke in like the police officer suggested? She shivered at the thought of him being in the house and hiding.

"Declan?"

"What is it?" His rough tone told Laci he wasn't in a good mood.

"I'm sorry," Laci began crying, "I'm so sorry. This

is all my fault."

"How is this your fault? Hey stop crying Laci. This is not your fault. Some guy broke in…how's that your fault?"

"He broke in because of me."

Declan shook his head and frowned as he hugged his sister. "Don't worry Laci. It's gonna be okay. I promise."

Laci nodded but she didn't believe him. She had a feeling that from now on, things were just going to get worse.

"Henry! We have to see Dr. Cummings this Saturday. Did you finish your journal?" Portia called out to her husband who was downstairs working on some random art project in his study. She was in their bedroom putting laundry away. As she was about to leave the room, she noticed a small key on the nightstand by Henry's side of the bed. She picked it up and looked at the dresser drawer he always kept locked.

Portia looked around and quickly unlocked the drawer. Inside was a small journal. "Why would he hide this?"

She placed his journal with hers to take to their appointment on Saturday. "If I don't do this he'll forget it like always."

Kay, Amber, and Laci sat at their local Red Robin gorging on the bottomless fries.

"So Laci...are you going to tell us what's going on with the dark circles under your eyes?" Kay asked. "It looks like you were up all night. It wouldn't have anything to do with that handsome co-worker of yours would it?"

"Someone broke into my house last night."

Amber and Kay stared at Laci in disbelief. Amber put down her burger and looked at Laci, "So why are you just telling us this now? That's not news you wait to tell your friends."

"Sorry," Laci murmured, "It was a rough night and Declan got hurt."

"Your brother was hurt? Is he okay? Are you okay? Did they take anything?"

Laci shook her head, "He's got a black eye. They didn't take anything. It was just a crazy night."

Kay nodded, "I'm sorry Laci but I'm glad you're okay."

Laci gave a weak smile, "It's fine. My brother wants to install a security system."

"That's a great idea," Kay looked at Amber, "Don't you think so?"

"Yeah...of course it is. Alarms that automatically call the police are great in case you can't call them yourself."

"Amber...I've been meaning to ask you...did you date a police officer before and not tell us?" Laci asked.

Amber looked surprised, "What?"

"What? Amber hid a boyfriend from us?" Kay laughed.

Amber blushed and shook her head, "Of course not."

"So you never dated an Officer Bishop before?" Laci asked.

Amber looked uncomfortable, "Why are you asking me this Laci?"

"I'm just curious. I met him."

Amber coughed, "No. I don't know him."

"Are you sure? Because he seemed to know you Amber."

Kay looked puzzled, "That's weird. Why would he say he went out with Amber if they didn't date?"

"I don't know," Amber shrugged, "Maybe he has me confused with someone else."

Kay didn't let it go, "You don't get confused about the people you date. Are you keeping secrets Ms. Gabriella?"

Amber tossed her napkin over her food, "Why do you keep asking? I told you I didn't date him. He must be confused. I'm going to the bathroom. Excuse me."

"You want me to come with you?" Kay asked.

"No," Amber noticed she was a bit too vehement in her answer so she answered again, "No...it's okay. Thanks. I'll be right back."

Laci couldn't help but notice how upset Amber looked.

"What was that about?" Kay asked Laci once Amber left them.

"I don't know but it seemed strange. Officer Bishop asked me to help him get back together with her...but she's telling us she never dated him."

"It's weird...but maybe he did get her confused with someone else."

Laci looked at Kay and asked, "Hey are things okay with you? I mean you're not having any problems are you?"

Kay laughed, "No. Why?"

Laci shrugged, "No reason...but if you ever have any problems...it doesn't matter what...you know you can come to me, right?"

Kay smiled, "Of course I do and the same goes for you. You, me, and Amber...we've been best friends since college. Marie Ann's gone but we're all important to each other."

Laci smiled. Kay was right. They were all important to one another. She thought of Amber who was still in the bathroom. Laci wondered, "Why did she deny dating Officer Joe Bishop? Did he lie or was she lying?"

Amber looked visibly upset when Laci mentioned Officer Bishop. There was more to this story than Amber was letting on and one thing was definitely clear. Kay, Amber, and Laci may be best friends...but they all had secrets.

CHAPTER 14

Amber sat across from her ex-boyfriend, Officer Joe Bishop. She adjusted her posture against the red pleather seat at their local Ihop. Joe was smiling at her, "Did you want me to order you your favorite? Blueberry pancakes?"

Amber frowned, "I don't eat those anymore. Listen Joe, I called you here so we could talk."

"What did you want to talk about?"

Not one to mince words, she got straight to her point, "Are you going around looking up my friends?"

"What? What are you talking about?"

Amber sneered, "Please Joe. I know how you are. Did you tell Laci that I was your girlfriend?"

"Laci? You asked me to meet you here because of her?"

Amber nodded, "Why else would I ask you to meet with me?"

"Oh I don't know…maybe to talk about our relationship?"

Amber sighed, "What relationship? We used to go out. Emphasis on the words used to."

"You seriously don't want to give us a second chance?"

"Why would I Joe? I told you I don't want to date an officer."

"Why? Because your friend told you that dating a cop was stressful?"

"That's not what she said Joe. I asked her how to deal with the stress of dating an officer. She told me it was something I would have to get used to and accept. I didn't want to accept it so we broke up. End of story."

"No, we didn't break up. You dumped me."

"Stop splitting hairs Joe. Laci just helped me work things out about what I did and didn't want in a relationship."

Joe gave a bitter laugh, "It always comes back to Laci. Why are you so obsessed with her?"

Amber laughed, "I'm not obsessed with her. She's my friend. Of course I care about her and what she thinks."

Joe snorted, "Yeah? Well I was your boyfriend and you didn't seem to care about what I thought. I should've known better than to think you wanted to get back together."

"Yeah you should have."

"When did you become such a bi-?"

Amber stopped him from calling her a curse word, "Don't even go there Joe. We broke up and I only wanted to meet you to tell you to stop bugging Laci."

"Is that what she told you? That I'm bugging her?"

"Does it matter? We aren't getting back together. Leave my friends alone."

"God, why did you even date me if you hate me so much?"

"I don't hate you Joe."

Joe reached his hand across the table to try and grasp hers, "You don't?"

Amber quickly moved her hand out of his reach, "No, I don't. What I feel for you is something like…"

Joe smiled, "Love?"

"Indifference."

Laci drove to the computer store to pick up her laptop. She had been a bit jumpy lately and even started paying attention to the cars that appeared in her rearview mirror's reflection. She was becoming paranoid that someone might start following her. As she pulled into the parking lot, she looked for a spot that wasn't surrounded by other cars. She ended up parking at the far end of the parking lot.

As she made her way to the computer repair counter, she scanned the faces of the customers to see if any of them were familiar. For all she knew her stalker was here at the store with her.

"May I help you?" a young man with a nametag that read "Marco" asked her. He had long hair pulled back in a ponytail and a faint mustache that looked like a smudge of dirt.

"Hi Marco, I'm here because I'm supposed to pick up my laptop."

"Name?"

"Laci Cummings."

His eyes squinted as if the name sounded familiar to

him. Laci wondered if he listened to her radio show.

"I'll be right back," Marco said as he left her waiting at the counter for a few minutes.

"Okay ma'am, we cleaned it up for you. It had a pretty nasty virus on it so we installed new antivirus software on it. You know you're supposed to update your virus protection software every year, don't you?"

Laci didn't know that, "Oh...I thought it stayed current on its own."

Marco shook his head in dismay, "I have customers come in here all the time and they don't realize that new viruses are created every day. Old software isn't advanced enough to protect your electronics. You need to update your software all the time."

"So which virus did I have on my computer?"

"A pretty scary one. It has a lot of different names. It's a spying program that allows hackers to watch their victims."

Laci nodded. This was something she was aware of. "Is it gone?"

Marco nodded, "Yes, but you should still be careful about what videos you're clicking on. Sometimes a link on Facebook or in an e-mail can install it again."

"Okay, thank you." Laci paid Marco who scratched his head as though he were thinking. "You seem really familiar," Marco said. "Have you come in here before?"

"No, this was my first computer repair."

Marco looked at the receipt's signature and smiled, "You're Dr. Cummings? Dr. Cummings the advice columnist, right?"

Laci smiled, "I give relationship advice for the newspaper and am on the radio show Love Guru."

"Wow that's so cool! My girlfriend loves your show.

She only went out with me after you told her that she should try dating someone different. She used to only date athletic men and I'm not exactly athletic."

"That's wonderful," Laci replied, "I'm happy to hear that. Normally people tell me that I'm the cause of their girlfriend breaking up with them but I'm glad I was able to help you in your relationship."

After Laci walked out of the store, she couldn't help feeling good about herself. She scanned the parking lot and spotted her car. Parked next to it was a large white van. It was old and dirty. It had a door on the side that probably slid open.

"Great," Laci mumbled facetiously under her breath as images of being shoved into the van ran through her head. Her pace slowed as she looked around the parking lot. She doubted anyone would even notice her being abducted into what she imagined as a dream vehicle for kidnappers everywhere.

She took a deep breath, "Chill out Laci. It's just a van. Just a creepy van that parked next to your car even though there are about a million empty spots closer to the store."

She walked to her car and cautiously placed her hand on the door handle.

The sound of the van's side door sliding open startled her, and she gave a frightened yelp.

A few kids began laughing as they scrambled out of the van. Laci had her back to her car with her hand over her chest.

She was becoming paranoid.

When she finally got home, a car she didn't recognize was parked in her driveway. As she walked inside, she saw her brother Declan talking with his friend Robert.

"Hey Laci, Robert's here."

Laci smiled, "Thank you Captain Obvious and hello Robert."

Robert laughed, "You two act like kids sometimes."

Declan shrugged then looked at Laci, "Robert works at a security company. He's going to help us install an alarm system."

"Really? I didn't know that Robert."

Robert grinned, "Yeah. I've worked there for a few years. I was telling Declan he wouldn't get so many shiners if he had an alarm system installed."

Declan touched his black eye and grimaced, "Yeah...this black eye is stopping me from getting dates."

Laci laughed, "Sure. Blame it on the black eye."

Robert laughed and Declan frowned. "I swear if that guy tries to break in again...it's on like King Kong."

"So are you paying for the security system Declan?" Robert asked his friend which gained Laci' attention.

"Yes, Declan, are you paying for this security system?" Laci repeated.

Declan pretended to huff and answered, "I'm not some homeless drifter. I work. I can afford it." He looked at his friend Robert and whispered, "How much is it?"

"If you install the upgraded package, the installation and two cameras are free but the price per month is a little less than sixty dollars."

"We get cameras?" Declan asked.

"Yeah, you can watch the house from your smart phone or laptop...whichever you like."

Declan whistled, "That sounds pretty high tech."

Laci thought of the virus in her computer and how technology was helping to scare her, "I'm not sure if we need something that fancy Robert. An alarm system with just a code key should be enough."

"Are you sure?" Robert asked looking from her to Declan.

"I'm sure. Declan, you don't have to pay for it. I will."

"Laci, I can pay for the alarm system. Besides I live here too."

Robert stopped them before they got into an argument, "You can always upgrade later if you want to. Laci, how about you and I discuss the installation?"

Laci nodded, and placed her laptop down.

"You picked up your laptop. Did they fix it?" her brother asked.

"Yeah. They also installed new virus protection so I think I'll be okay."

Declan and Laci continued talking about the laptop while Robert stared at it.

"Hey man are you okay?" Declan asked his friend.

"Huh? Oh…sorry, my mind drifted off for a minute. Yeah I'm fine."

"Still thinking about your ex?"

"What?" Robert asked, embarrassed.

"Hey there's no shame in getting dumped. If you need help, ask Laci. She's a love doctor remember?"

Laci smiled at Robert, "I'd be happy to listen if you ever want to talk Robert."

Declan interjected, "Just don't forget to return the favor by way of a discount on the security alarm."

Robert laughed while Laci punched her brother in the arm and chastised him, "Stop being King Kong."

After the three of them had decided on a date to install the alarm system, Laci walked upstairs.

It had been a few days since the break-in and she was still paranoid. She looked around her room, taking in the familiar dresser, nightstands, and lamps. She was amazed that just a few days ago, everything in the room had felt foreign to her.

"I can still see you."

Laci turned around to look at the doorway. No one was there. She wasn't sure if she had heard anything. Did someone just whisper to her? A few minutes had passed but she didn't hear the voice a second time.

"Laci!"

She jumped and turned around to see her brother and Robert standing in the doorway.

"We're going to pick up some burgers. You want one?"

"Uh…yeah. Get me a cheeseburger."

"You got it."

After Declan and Robert left, Laci sat on her bed and couldn't help but wonder if she was going crazy.

CHAPTER 15

Laci was trying to wrap her head around the fact that it was already Friday and tonight was her date with Andrew. She looked over at him. He turned his head to face her and winked, causing her to quickly look away.

"Ahh the chemistry between you two is too cute. I could take some pictures and put them on the show's website. I think the female listeners would eat it up. Dr. Cummings the love guru snatches herself a sexy psychologist."

"I'm not sure how I feel about you calling me a sexy psychologist."

George waved a hand at him in dismissal, "It's not the forties Andrew. I can call you sexy and it's not weird at all."

"Really? Because it feels a little weird to me since you're my boss," Andrew laughed, "Besides, we're just going on one date. It's a bit too premature to try and advertise us as a couple."

"Couple?" Laci asked in surprise. She wasn't sure what was going on with George but she didn't like it. She stood up, "Okay…well this has been fun but playtime is over. George, you need to cut the celebrity dating crap out or I swear I'll cancel this date."

"What?" Andrew asked, clearly not expecting her to say that.

George also stood up, "Hey now...no need to get over excited Laci. I'm just kidding...I would never do anything to jeopardize this show or the synergy you two share."

"I don't care George. I agreed to go on a date with Dr. Brett but I can just as easily change my mind."

An uncomfortable silence filled the room after Laci spoke.

"Well...this is awkward. I'll just leave you two alone for a few minutes," George said as he gathered his notepad and some pens. He sneaked a glance at Andrew and mouthed, "Good luck."

Andrew chose to ignore George and as soon as he was alone with Laci, asked, "Is something wrong Laci? Listen, I'm sorry if you felt pressured into going on a date with me. I know the segment had to deal with co-workers dating. If you think it's not a good idea...we can always cancel it."

Laci listened to Andrew giver her an out and she frowned. She wished she didn't suffer from verbal diarrhea and hadn't just threatened to cancel her date with Andrew. She really couldn't, even if she wanted to. Her stalker had made sure of that. He wanted her to ask Andrew out on the air or he would hurt her friend Kay.

Laci hadn't heard from her harasser in a couple of days. It was oddly quiet and for some reason it had made her more apprehensive than usual. She looked at Andrew and faked a smile, "No. I'm sorry. I don't want to break our date. It's just George is so gung-ho about this couple thing that it just surprised me. That's all. I don't like people trying to tell me what to do."

"Don't worry Laci. I'm not trying to rush to be in a relationship with you…or anyone for that matter. I'd love to spend some time with you. Maybe get to know you a little better. I think you're an incredible woman and I'm surprised you're still single."

Laci couldn't help but give a genuine smile, "I could say the same for you."

"That I'm an incredible woman?" Laci laughed in response and he went on, "Since we're done for the day…I guess I'll see you later?"

She nodded. Their show had already ended, giving her thirty minutes to get ready. Earlier, Andrew had warned her not to worry about dressing up.

"Are we going to McDonalds? Because that wouldn't be my worst first date."

Andrew just shrugged and answered, "Don't wear anything you wouldn't mind tossing."

She wasn't sure how to take that. Was he trying to be sexual? If he was, he was failing. She decided to go with turquoise skinny jeans, a loose sleeveless off-white top, and some cute wedges. She decorated her outfit with a gold bangle necklace and a bohemian turquoise bracelet.

She was at home waiting for her date when she heard someone give a wolf whistle. She turned around to see her brother Declan.

"Does someone have a date or are you playing dress up?" Declan asked.

"With Dr. Brett?"

"Yes. Why do you ask?"

Declan shrugged, "No reason. I like him. I think you two would make a good fit and not just because you're both shrink wraps."

"Declan, I told you we're not shrinks."

"Yeah…yeah. Anyway, I hope you have fun tonight. You deserve it after everything that's been going on."

Laci smiled at Declan. She knew he was worried about her. She noticed that he would check on her several times a day. He probably had no idea that his simple, "Everything okay sis?" meant the world to her.

"Thanks. Declan. I'm not sure where we're going but he said not to dress too fancy." Declan was going to respond when the doorbell rang.

"I bet that's him!"

"I'll leave you to it. Have fun tonight." Declan quickly ran upstairs and Laci took a deep breath and opened the door.

Andrew was standing on the other side wearing black pants and a dress shirt and of course topping it off in the ever famous hat. In his hands he carried a dozen long-stemmed red roses.

"Oh Andrew! Are those for me?"

"No, they're for your brother. Where is he?"

Laci chuckled and reached out to take the roses, "Oww!"

"What's wrong?" Andrew asked.

"The stems have thorns. One of them poked me."

Andrew gently took her finger in his hand and inspected it, "It's just bleeding a little."

Laci realized, as she put the flowers in a vase, that she had never felt Andrew's hands that way before; they were so gentle. Twenty minutes later, they were seated in a fancy restaurant across town.

"You said not to dress up," Laci admonished him.

"You look perfect so don't worry about it."

As they waited for their food, Laci looked around at

the other patrons. She wondered if her stalker had followed her and Andrew. As dinner progressed she started to feel comfortable with Andrew. He told her stories about his childhood and his family. She shared stories about her friends and working with George. Before Laci realized it, she felt relaxed.

"Is there anything else I can get you two?" the waitress asked.

They both answered in the negative and as she walked away, Laci noticed someone out of the corner of her eye. A man sitting at a nearby table with a menu covering most of his face. What she thought was strange was that he was wearing sunglasses indoors. Laci picked up her phone and turned the camera on. She switched it to selfie mode and faced the camera towards the man. She had the phone angled to make it seem as though she was looking at herself. In reality she was watching him. She could've sworn she saw a camera from above his menu.

"Is something wrong Laci?"

She looked at Andrew and whispered, "Don't look, but do you see that man in the sunglasses?"

Andrew laughed, "How can I see if you told me not to look?"

"Just be stealthy," Laci whispered in frustration.

Andrew grinned and pretended to drop a spoon. He bent down to pick it up and looked at the man wearing sunglasses. "What the heck? You're right."

"What did you see?"

"I think he's watching us."

Laci nodded. Chased called the waitress over to pay the check and as they both got up, Laci noticed the man in sunglasses was gone.

She turned over to Andrew, "He's gone. Did you see

him leave?"

He shook his head, "Let's just go."

As they walked to Andrew's car, Laci felt uncomfortable. She looked around her and was surprised to see a man standing behind a van close to where Andrew was parked.

"Andrew," Laci whispered.

He looked in the direction of her gaze and saw the man from the restaurant. The man quickly raised his phone, and snapped a picture. Laci gasped and the man knew he had been caught. He started to run but Andrew began racing after him.

"Stop right there!" Andrew yelled. Laci slipped out of her shoes and began running after them. She tossed her wedge shoe at the man's head, hitting him, and causing him to stop for a second. Andrew was able to eventually tackle the guy to the ground. The two wrestled for a moment. Laci came running as best she could, picking up her shoe and placing both of them back on.

Andrew had the man pinned down to the cold cement.

"Who are you?" Laci asked. "Why are you stalking us?"

The man choked out an answer, "Some guy paid me to do it."

"Paid you?" Andrew asked.

The man attempted to nod, "Yeah. He gave me fifty bucks and said to take as many photos as I could."

"What was his name?" Andrew asked.

"I don't remember. He just said to e-mail him the pictures and he'd wire me the money."

"What was his e-mail address?" Laci asked.

"junglegeorge@loveguru.com," the man groaned.

Laci fumed when she heard the name, "I'm going to kill George when I see him!"

Andrew laughed and let the guy he had tackled get up. "Listen, I don't know why he hired you, but I wouldn't share those pictures you took tonight."

The man rubbed his shoulder where it had been slammed into the ground, "Fine. I won't send them to Jungle George. Instead I'll just save them."

Andrew was about to respond when Laci shook her head, "Don't even think about it. Give me your camera or I'll have my friend here throw you back onto the ground." He looked from Laci to Andrew and surrendered his camera. They allowed the man with the camera to leave after deleting his photos.

"Well that was a definite killjoy," Laci muttered.

Andrew was driving his car and she noticed he wasn't driving in the direction of her home, "Andrew, where are we going?"

He turned over to her and smiled, "I have a surprise."

"A surprise? What kind of surprise?"

Andrew pulled off onto an old country road, "Do you trust me Laci?"

"Andrew, I hate it when people ask me that. If you have to ask you know I don't."

He laughed and agreed, "You're right. Trust is communicating without speech."

"So where exactly are we going?"

Andrew laughed wildly, startling Laci. His speed increased as he drove forward.

"Andrew slow down!"

He didn't listen, but turned his floodlights on to illuminate the road ahead of him.

"Don't worry about my driving skills, I am a stunt

driver in another life."

"Andrew. I'm serious slow down!"

Still Laci was ignored. Andrew continued to look forward when he asked, "Laci I really think you're going to enjoy this. I wasn't sure if you would but after seeing you with that man earlier...you're tough enough."

"Tough enough? Tough enough for what?"

Andrew smirked, "Mayhem."

"What the heck are you talking about Andrew? You don't sound like yourself. What is it that you want to do exactly?"

"What do I want to do? It's not that Laci. This is something I want both of us to do. Did you know that most first dates are only successful if the couple has a date where they do some kind of activity together as opposed to just having dinner and seeing a movie?"

"You want us to do something together?" Laci asked, trying to make sense of what he was saying.

"Yes."

"Okay what exactly do you want us to do tonight?" Laci asked.

Andrew turned his eyes away from the road and looked at Laci. She was frightened and was gripping her purse. She needed to inconspicuously get her cellphone and call for help.

"Don't be scared Laci. I'm not going to ask you to do something that I don't think you can't handle."

Laci looked out at the road and back to Andrew. She placed her hand in her bag and felt for her phone while continuing to speak to Andrew, "What is it that you think I can handle?"

Andrew turned back to the road before answering in

a clear and distinct voice.
"Murder."

CHAPTER 16

"Murder?" Laci felt for her phone and tried pulling it out without Andrew noticing.

Andrew grinned and sped forward to an old building. There were a few cars parked out front.

"Where are we?" Laci asked.

"This place belongs to a friend of mine." Andrew parked his car and ordered Laci to get out, "What are you waiting for?"

"I don't want to be here," Laci whispered.

"What?"

"I don't want to be here," she said in a stronger voice. "I want to go home."

Andrew looked disappointed, "I'm sorry Laci but we need to do this."

"No we don't. We really don't," Laci pleaded.

"Are you scared?" Andrew asked before getting out and walking to her side of the car. She locked her door and he laughed, pressing the button on his keys that unlocked the car. He opened her door and she struggled against him as he tried helping her out.

"What's the matter with you Laci?" Andrew asked laughing.

"Get away from me!"

Andrew suddenly let go and stepped back, "What's

going on Laci?"

"You tell me Andrew? Why are you all of a sudden talking about murdering people?"

A moment of silence passed between the two of them and Andrew just stared at Laci in disbelief.

A big truck came up the road with several teens in the back. They were hollering and laughing.

"I love paintball. Get ready to die Frank!" one of the teens shouted to the driver. They all ran through the entrance of the old looking building.

"Do you know where we are?" Andrew asked Laci.

She shook her head in confusion.

Andrew pointed up to the faded paint on the side of the wooden building. It was barely noticeable but if you looked closely, you could see it.

Murder by Paintball

"Paintball," Andrew answered. He shook his head in disappointment and made a tsking sound. He turned his back to Laci and spoke, "I brought you here because I know you've been stressed lately and I thought shooting people full of paint would make you feel better. Relieve some stress."

"Oh my God. I'm sorry Andrew…I just-"

Andrew turned to face her, "You just what? Thought I really wanted to murder people? Why would you think that? Have I ever done anything to make you believe I'm some kind of psychopath?"

Laci immediately became defensive, "Well why did you say we were going to murder people? Sane people don't' say things like that!"

"This place is called *Murder by Paintball*. The slogan is *Death by Paint*. It was a joke!"

"Well it wasn't funny!" Laci fidgeted in her seat. She was embarrassed. "I guess we should just go home."

"You really don't want to try it?" Andrew asked.

"The paintball? I don't know how. I've never played paintball before."

Andrew sighed, "I'm not going to lie…I'm still offended that you thought I was a murderer. Still, I can't let you live the rest of your life without experiencing a good round of paintball. Rule number one: it's just paintball. We don't say play paintball. Got it?"

Laci giggled, causing Andrew to ask, "What's so funny?"

"Lots of things. How dumb I was a few minutes ago, that you're way too into this paintball stuff, and that I almost called the cops on you."

Andrew laughed, "Yeah that would have been bad. Funny…but bad."

"This is an interesting idea though. It's different," Laci smiled.

"Different good or different bad."

"Different good. So how did you know I was stressed?"

"Your brother called me. He knew we were going on a date and suggested it."

Laci laughed, "My brother told you to take me out to paintball?"

"Well actually, he told me to take you to a bar in the next town that lets you do mud wrestling…but I told him it probably wouldn't be a good idea."

"Good call," Laci laughed. "Either way, thank you. I have been stressed by a lot of things lately."

"Well you're lucky enough to have a highly sought after psychologist at your disposal if you want to talk about it."

Laci squinted her eyes as if she were in deep thought, "Highly sought after huh? How do I know you're really good at giving advice or not?"

Andrew looked away and smiled, "Well...I do have my own radio show."

"Your own radio show?" she emphasized the word own.

"Well I share it with another doctor but she's just there to be eye candy."

Laci laughed, "Didn't you say it was a radio show? No one would even see her."

Andrew laughed, "Oh that's right. Well I guess she's only eye candy to me since I'm the only one that's lucky enough to see her."

Laci blushed and looked down to hide her face.

Andrew smiled and grabbed her hand to drag her inside the building. Laci was in awe at what she saw. Teens and adults were dressed in dark suits and goggles.

"Are we able to play in the dark?" Laci asked.

"Of course. It's more fun that way," Andrew answered.

Laci regretted not wearing flats but decided to make the best of it. After they were dressed, the man working at the counter handing out paintball guns told them, "Don't worry, it's a lot of fun and doesn't hurt a bit."

Laci doubted that but took her paint gun. Andrew taught her how to use the gun and the two of them prepared for paint battle. Laci was happy that she had joined Andrew. She was having so much fun, shooting strangers with paint and running behind standing boards to hide. It was exhilarating. She imagined each person she shot was her stalker.

An hour later, they were on their way to Laci's house.

"My cheeks hurt from smiling so much. Thank you Andrew."

"Are you kidding? I got to see the beautiful Laci Cummings shoot strangers with a paint gun. People should pay money for that. You were vicious!"

Laci couldn't help but giggle at herself. She was happy and she hadn't felt so relaxed in weeks. They reached her house and Andrew walked her to the door.

"Normally, I would try to kiss you goodnight but after seeing you shoot people with paintballs, I'm not sure if I should risk it," Andrew told her.

"Well that's too bad. I don't normally kiss during first dates but I was willing to make an exception."

"Is that so?"

Laci whispered, "Maybe."

Andrew began to lean in but they both jumped at the sound of a horn honking. They looked towards the street to see two teenagers driving past laughing. One of them stuck their head out of the window and shouted, "Get a room!"

Laci and Andrew laughed, "Talk about bad timing," Andrew muttered. Laci lightly pushed him back.

"Thank you for the date Andrew. I had a lot of fun." She gave him a quick peck on the cheek and smiled at him as she unlocked her front door and went inside.

Andrew was smiling up until she closed the door to her home. Laci was fortunate that she had closed the door and was unable to see Andrew's smile turn into an angry frown.

"Declan I have groceries in the car. Go get them!" Laci was carrying plastic grocery bags in her hands as she walked into the kitchen. Sitting on one of her counter stools was Robert, Declan' friend.

"Robert! What are you doing here?"

"I'm moving in," he casually answered.

"What?"

Robert laughed, "I'm here to visit Declan Laci. Why else would I be here?"

Laci gave him the stink eye and answered, "Oh I don't know…maybe installing a security alarm."

Robert grabbed an apple from her groceries, "I told Declan it was scheduled to be installed on Monday."

"Really? He didn't say a word to me."

"That's Dec for you."

"Where is my brother?" Laci asked.

"Taking a shower. His black eye finally faded enough that he wants to meet up with some women I know." Robert explained.

"Well good luck with that but in the meantime, will you be a sweetheart and get the groceries from my car?"

Robert looked surprised but did as he was asked.

A few minutes later, Declan came downstairs, "Sorry to make you wait Robert."

Laci looked at her brother and his friend, "What time are you two leaving?"

"Are you trying to kick us out?" Declan joked.

"I have clients today Declan. You and Robert have got to go."

"Kicking me out of my own home so that she can

see some wackadoos," Declan shook his head.

The doorbell rang and Laci looked at both of them, "Give me ten minutes and then leave." She ran to the front door and opened it to see Andrew.

"Andrew! What are you doing here?" she asked looking past him for Portia and Henry Meiser who were her expected clients for the day.

"I'm sorry to show up unexpectedly. Are you expecting someone else?"

"Sorry, I'm waiting for some clients. Come in but don't stay long. Oh sorry...that was rude."

Andrew laughed, "Don't worry I understand."

"Andrew!" Laci and Andrew looked to see Declan standing behind them. "How was the date last night? Did you get to third base?"

Laci punched Declan in the arm, "Stop being gross."

He laughed and all three of them went back to the kitchen. Laci looked at the three handsome men in her house and told all of them to leave, "Seriously, you guys need to go."

The doorbell rang again, "That's them. I promise my clients their privacy so stay here and leave in ten minutes. Understand?"

All three men nodded and she smiled as she ran back to the front door.

Henry and Portia Meiser were an odd couple but Laci really felt she could help them. She opened the door and allowed them in.

"Dr. Cummings?" Henry asked as soon as he came inside, "Is it okay if I use the bathroom?"

"Henry! I told you to go when we were at home," his wife scolded him.

"I'm sorry Portia but I didn't have to go then,"

Henry apologized.

Laci gave a fake smile, "It's not a problem. Henry, there's a bathroom down the hall. Portia and I will be in the study waiting for you."

Henry nodded and walked towards the bathroom while Laci and Portia walked to her study.

"Dr. Cummings, I have the journals you wanted us to write in," Portia pulled out both journals.

"That's great. Let's wait for Henry to get back and we can begin reviewing them. Your first assignment was to write a letter to your spouse."

"Dr. Cummings, I'm paying for this hour, I don't want to waste it waiting for Henry. I'm starting now."

Laci tried stopping Portia but it was impossible. She pulled out Henry's journal and opened it up to the first page and began reading.

"Destiny. Our love is destiny. There was a time that I felt so lonely I would pray the Lord took my life. I couldn't stand the loneliness anymore. Then I met you and my whole life changed. I felt alive again. My hurt burst with joy," Portia began tearing up.

"Dr. Cummings can you believe Henry is so...so sentimental?" Portia asked. "I'm actually surprised. We've felt so distant. This is incredibly sweet."

She continued reading, "My heart screams in pain when we're apart and I know that someday we'll always be together forever. You are my love for life...Dr. Cummings."

Portia looked up from the journal to an ashen faced Laci. "This says Dr. Cummings. Are you having an affair with my husband?"

It was at that moment that Henry entered the study after using the bathroom. He saw an angry Portia and a pale Laci and asked, "What's going on in here?"

Portia turned to him with an expression of pure venom, "How dare you!" She threw the book at him, which he dodged.

Portia ran towards Henry and began pummeling him. Laci shouted for her to stop. Henry pushed Portia away who fell to the ground. She yelled, "You want to hit me? I won't let you get away with this Henry!" She jumped up and began picking up whatever was around her and tossed it at Henry.

"Stop it right now!" Laci yelled only to get the attention of Portia who began throwing things at her too.

"I hate you! You're fired you husband stealer!"

Laci shrieked when Portia tossed a glass figurine at her. Henry shouted at his wife, "Stop it Portia. It's not her fault that I love her!"

"Love? You love her?" Portia was livid. She turned back to Laci, "Let's see how much you love her when I disfigure her face!"

"No!" Henry ran forward and hit his wife, knocking her out. Laci screamed and the door burst open.

"Andrew!" Laci was relieved to see Andrew standing at the door with his phone to his ear, "I'm calling 911 so don't anybody move."

Thirty minutes later the police had picked up Henry and the ambulance picked up Portia who would later be taken to jail as well. Laci and Andrew had both given statements. Laci sat amidst the rubble of her once tidy study.

"Can you believe this?" she asked Andrew who handed her a beer.

"It's not uncommon for a client to fall for his psychologist," Andrew replied.

"Yeah but I saw his journal. It was so disturbing. At

least it should all be over now."

"What should be over?"

Laci didn't want to elaborate. She hoped Henry would finally stop stalking her and this nightmare she had been living the past few weeks would be over. She had mentioned her friend's murder to the police and they told her they would check if he had an alibi for that night. Laci was grateful to Andrew for staying behind after her brother and Robert had left the house.

After Andrew left, Laci walked upstairs to an awful sight. On her bed were the roses that Andrew had given her the night prior. They were cut up into small pieces and the red rose petals looked like giant drops of blood against her white bedspread.

Amber sat in front of her computer. She was browsing the Love Guru website. Pictures of psychologists Laci Cummings and Andrew Brett were splashed all over the screen.

Amber was on her cellphone, "Don't tell me what to do. I have everything under control. Yeah…yeah whatever you say. Listen I'm busy. I'll call you later."

Amber rolled her eyes when she hung up the phone and snorted as she read the comments about Laci and Andrew.

Her face contorted into an ugly expression as she poised her hands above the keyboard and typed, "Laci Cummings is a fraud. She needs to leave Dr. Brett alone. I HATE HER!!!"

☐

CHAPTER 17

"What are you typing Amber?" Kay asked as she peered over her friend's shoulder. She was shocked at the words on the computer screen.

"Laci Cummings is a fraud. She needs to leave Dr. Brett alone. I HATE HER!!!"

"Uh...Abbs?"

Amber was trying to come up with another comment to type out. She looked back at Kay, "What?"

"When George called and asked that we get listeners riled up about Laci and Andrew, I don't think he meant in a negative way."

Amber and Kay had met George two years ago at a party Laci was hosting. He was a bit unconventional but passionate about his job. Once he had found out that Marie Ann, Amber, Kay, and Laci were best friends, he saved all of their numbers and would occasionally text them about upcoming events the radio station was having. Yesterday he had bribed both Amber and Kay into helping him promote Laci and Andrew as a couple in exchange for some concert tickets.

"He said to get people talking," Amber lightly tapped her fingers against the keyboard.

"He didn't say to start rumors. Delete it Amber. I can't believe you typed that in the first place."

"Fine," Amber muttered, "Marie Ann would have sided with me." She deleted her post about hating Laci.

Kay scoffed, "No she wouldn't have."

Amber ignored that comment, "What about something about her being pregnant? Or a secret marriage?"

Kay covered her face in her hands, "Oh I can't believe we agreed to do this for some Maroon 5 tickets."

"Kay, they're front row tickets! Besides, we're helping Laci and her show become more popular."

Kay groaned, "We're probably going to Hell in the section for bad friends for this. Write the one about the secret marriage."

Amber giggled, "But why would they keep their marriage a secret?"

Kay contemplated that, "Fine, scratch that. Ooh I know! Type out that they're secretly engaged!"

Amber and Kay locked eyes and both of them smiled and said, "Perfect."

"What in the world?" Laci was in her study, reading her e-mails. She was getting an influx of congratulations in regards to her recent engagement to Dr. Andrew Brett.

"Hey sis," Declan came strolling into her study, a tablet in his hands, "Are you getting married?"

"What?" Laci was surprised even Declan was aware of the engagement rumor.

Declan showed her his tablet which had the local society page up. Laci groaned, "This isn't in the newspaper is it?"

Declan shook his head and answered, "No. This is too new so it's just online. Are you and Andrew engaged?"

"Yeah right Declan. Do you actually think I would get engaged and not tell you?"

Declan shrugged, "I don't know. It kind of hurt my feelings...thinking you would keep it a secret from me. This sounds bad but I'm glad you're still one of those old single crazy cat ladies that no one will marry."

He grinned and Laci scowled, "First of all, I'm not old. Second...I don't have any cats!"

"But you admit to the crazy part, right?"

"Declan!"

He smirked and walked forward, wrapping Laci in an unexpected hug, "I'm sorry Laci. I just...I just want you to be happy and safe."

"Where is this coming from all of a sudden? Are you okay Declan?" Laci asked.

Declan released her and gave a soft smile, "I'm fine. I just want you safe."

Laci cocked her head to one side and studied her brother, "Are you on drugs?"

He laughed, "What? I can't care about my sister?"

"Of course you can. But what's with all the 'I want you safe' talk?"

Declan shook his head, "Nothing. It's just with everything that's been going on like the break in, Marie Ann's death, and now your crazy clients…I just want you safe."

"Well you'll be happy to know that I came to a decision yesterday regarding my practice."

"What?"

"I think I'm going to rent an office to see clients in. After what happened yesterday, I don't' want to take the chance of them invading my personal space anymore." Laci didn't tell Declan about the cut up roses she found on her bed. She figured it was another prank of Henry's.

"My sister is finally seeing the light! Did you want me to go with you to look for your new office space?"

"No thanks. Andrew already recommended a location to me."

"And we're back to Andrew," Declan smiled. "Did you just blush Laci? Is my sister blushing?"

Laci laughed, "I'm not blushing! I'm too old to blush about a guy."

"Ahh so you admit you're old?" Declan said wiggling his eyebrows up and down, causing Laci to lightly hit him on the arm.

"I'm not old!"

Declan laughed and changed the subject, "So did you hear anything about that Henry Meiser guy?"

Laci shook her head, "Not yet. The police are supposed to keep me updated. Can you imagine? If he's been the guy sending me notes, weird texts, and worst of all the person that killed Marie Ann?"

"Don't dwell on it too much Laci. There's no way you could've known."

Laci was going to respond when her cell phone rang.

It was George. As soon as she picked up, he began talking, "Listen Laci. I did it for the show. I'm really sorry but your fans are eating it up, right now."

"Are you also responsible for all of the engagement rumors, George?"

He didn't respond and Laci groaned, "George how could you? I'm pretty sure this is some sort of harassment. And what were you thinking about...getting some creep to follow me and Andrew around on our date? I thought someone was stalking us! Do you know how scary that was?"

"I'm sorry Laci. I wanted pictures for the website. It doesn't matter anyway since you two deleted everything he had."

"If you do something like that again- I don't care how long we've known each other George. I won't forgive you!"

"Okay...okay. I won't use anymore subterfuge to promote your relationship."

"George, I'm serious," Laci warned.

She could hear George sighing on the other end, "Fine! I won't hire people to secretly take your picture with Andrew anymore."

"People? Did you hire anyone else George?"

"What do you take me for Laci? Of course not. It was just the one guy and he failed. If there are any more relationship pictures floating around...it's not my doing."

Laci sighed and she and George disconnected the call.

"What was that about?" Declan asked.

Laci began rubbing small circles against her temple, "You don't want to know."

Declan chuckled and then changed the topic, "By

the way, I'm almost done cleaning the attic out. Are you sure you don't mind me using it as my studio?"

"Of course not. Did you find a lot of junk up there?"

Declan shrugged, "A lot of old papers, clothes, trophies…stuff like that."

"Old papers?"

"Yeah about our adoptions and newspaper clippings. Just stuff."

"Adoption papers aren't just stuff Declan. They're important."

"Well I have it all stored away. Just let me know if you need it."

They both walked to the kitchen and Declan rubbed his stomach, "All this talking has made me hungry. I'm gonna go pick up a pizza. Is that cool with you?" Laci nodded and Declan left the house.

A sense of relief washed over Laci as she thought of her stalker being behind bars. In actuality, Henry had probably already been released from police custody but at least now she had a face to the man that was harassing her. If he truly did hurt Marie Ann he would eventually be in jail and now Laci knew she had enough evidence to apply for a restraining order.

She thought of her conversation with Declan. He mentioned finding adoption papers in the attic. Laci wanted to see those papers. Fifteen minutes later, she walked upstairs and towards the attic's entrance. It was amazing. He had really cleaned the place up.

Laci walked over to his desk and rummaged through the drawers. A small part of her discouraged her, reminding her that this was her brother's space and she wouldn't appreciate him going through her office drawers.

She spotted an unlabeled box to the left of his desk and opened it up. It was full of papers. "Bingo," she whispered.

The corner of a bright gold envelope at the bottom of the box caught her attention. It was hidden behind a bunch of other papers but she was able to easily pull it out.

Her heart stopped as she recognized the familiar gold envelope. For a moment, she thought Declan had kept one of the envelopes her stalker had left. "No, those are still in my room," she reminded herself.

Laci slowly opened the envelope to find pictures. Pictures of her from the past few weeks. She gasped as she saw a picture of herself at Marie Ann's funeral. There was another picture of her having lunch with Kay, Marie Ann, and Amber. The last picture was of her and Andrew leaving the paintball place.

She instantly felt nauseous.

Why did Declan have these pictures?

She was so engrossed in the pictures, that she didn't see her brother standing in the doorway of the attic. She jumped when she saw him, "Declan!"

"What are you doing Laci?" his eyes were on the gold envelope in her hands.

"I was looking for the adoption papers. I found these," Laci explained holding up the gold envelope of pictures, "Declan did George hire you to take pictures of me?"

Declan slowly shook his head and walked forward, "No. George didn't hire me."

Laci took an unsteady step backward, "Then why do you have these pictures Declan?"

Declan took another step closer and asked, "Why do

you think?"

Laci didn't know what to think. As far as she knew, her world had just turned upside down.

CHAPTER 18

"Declan...why do you have these pictures?" Laci asked her brother who looked upset.

"Why were you going through my things Laci?"

She took a step back, "These are pictures of me Declan. The kind a stalker or some kind of sick voyeur would take. Why do you have them?"

"Why do you think?" he asked.

"I don't know what to think! It's why I'm asking!" she was breathing heavily in fear and anger but mostly anger. Laci couldn't believe that her brother would do something like this. It wasn't possible. There had to be some plausible explanation.

Declan stopped moving towards her when he saw how scared she was. She unconsciously had one of her hands up in case she needed to ward off an attack from him. He sighed and crouched down to the ground, keeping his face in his hands, "I'm such an idiot."

Laci stared at her brother in confusion, "Declan...you can talk to me. I'm your sister.

Whatever it is…we can work through this together. I can help you."

Declan laughed, still hiding his face in his hands, "Help me?"

"Yes, I can try to help you."

"Laci you can't even help yourself. How are you going to help me? Why do you think I'm even in this mess?" Declan had looked up to Laci and was shouting as he stood up.

Laci tossed the photos onto the desk and asked, "What exactly is going on? What situation?"

"Those pictures," Declan pointed to them, "They weren't taken by me Laci. They were given to me."

"Given to you?"

"I found them in my truck yesterday morning. There was also a note that said if I went to the police they'd kill you," Declan ran his hands in his hair.

Laci stared at her brother in disbelief, "What did he want?"

Declan looked up surprised, "How did you-"

"How did I know? Why else would he threaten to kill me if you went to the police? He wanted something. So what was it? What did he want?"

Declan shook his head, "I don't want to talk about it. It doesn't matter anymore anyway. They arrested that creepy client you have so we shouldn't be bothered by him anymore."

"They arrested him for domestic violence not for stalking or blackmailing. What did the note say?"

Declan shrugged, "It said to leave you in the house alone on Monday night."

"What? And you were going to do it?" Laci rushed forward and began hitting her brother who tried covering himself with his arms.

"Oww…stop it Laci! I wasn't going to leave you by yourself. Do you think I'm stupid or something?"

Laci stopped for a moment to respond, "You didn't tell me about the pictures as soon as you found them…so yeah!" She proceeded to hit him until he grabbed her wrists.

"Look I didn't know what to do alright? I freaked so I called Robert to come over and we talked about it. He was going to come in on Monday and install the alarm."

Laci attempted to hit him again, "Why didn't you tell me?"

"Because I didn't want you to get more scared than you already were. You just went on a date with that psychologist. It was the first time in weeks that you weren't walking around here on eggshells. How could I tell you that someone sent me their stalker photos of you?" Declan let go of her wrists and took a step back, "Admit it. If I told you about it…you would've been worse than you already are."

"I'm fine!" Laci said loudly to convince her brother but somehow it sounded more like she was trying to convince herself.

"Are you? Because you don't look fine," Declan whispered and swiped a tear from her cheek.

Her face crumpled as she leaned into her brother for support, "Why is this happening to me Declan? What did I do to deserve this?"

Declan patted her back as she sobbed against him, "It's okay Laci. That guy's in jail and the alarm will be installed soon. It's going to be okay. I promise."

"Tell me again where you were that night," the detective leaned forward against the wooden table that separated him and Henry Meiser.

"I told you I don't know that woman," Henry said as he pointed to the picture of Marie Ann Davis. "I wasn't even in town that week. I was out of town on a business trip."

"Is there anyone that can corroborate your story?" the detective asked.

"My story? Do you think I'm making this up?" Henry was insulted.

The detective leaned back and appraised Henry, "You're not a bad looking guy. You make a good amount of money. I bet women throw themselves at you."

Henry blushed, "I'm married!"

The detective shrugged, "So?"

"So I wouldn't...wouldn't do something like...like that," Henry said, clearly flustered.

"You wouldn't be the first to stray from the woman he's been married to for years. Besides, I saw that journal. You know...the one where you wrote all those love letters to your therapist."

"That was private!"

"C'mon Henry. Throw me a bone. How did you know Marie Ann Davis?"

Henry slammed his hands on the desk, "I didn't know her! I don't know her! I don't want to know her!"

"She was friends with your therapist...you know...the woman you claimed to love in your journal," the detective smirked.

Henry's eyes narrowed, "How dare you mock me. Those are my personal feelings that I wrote about!"

"I hate to break it to you but your Dr. Cummings wants nothing to do with you. She's probably filing a restraining order right about now."

"I haven't done anything! For the last time…I'm innocent."

The detective stood up, "I'll be right back Henry. You keep thinking of someone that saw you when you were out of town."

The detective walked out to see Officer Tracy Stewart waiting for him. "Did you find out anything?" she asked.

"Nope. Not a thing. Honestly Tracy, I don't think he's the guy."

Officer Tracy Stewart had told the detective in charge of Marie Ann Davis's murder all about the stalking of Dr. Cummings and how the same person could be the murderer of Marie Ann Davis. It was all connected but convoluted and Tracy wanted to get to the bottom of it. When Henry had been arrested for domestic violence, the journal he had written his love fantasies in was given to her by his wife Portia.

"Take it," she said, "I may need it back as evidence for when I divorce him."

At the time, Tracy just thanked Mrs. Meiser and shook her head at the entire situation.

"I'm sorry Tracy but we're going to have to let him go. There's not much evidence to show that he's the one that killed Marie Ann Davis other than the connection to this stalking business and that's pretty light to begin with. Besides, once he lawyers up, it'll be easy for him to miraculously come up with an alibi."

Tracy shook her head and thanked the detective. As she walked back to her desk, she spotted her partner Officer Joe Bishop, texting on his phone. He didn't look up when he said, "I told you it would be a waste of time."

Tracy nodded. Maybe Bishop was right. Maybe Dr. Laci Cummings really didn't have a stalker.

Laci was sitting in her living room next to her brother Declan. They were still drained from their argument earlier in the day.

"Are you still mad at me?" Declan asked.

Laci shook her head, "I'm not mad. I'm just disappointed that's all. I wish neither of us had to deal with this kind of thing."

Declan nodded. He was about to speak when the doorbell rang. Laci answered it to see Andrew with a box of pizza in his hands.

"What are you doing here?" she asked.

"Declan invited me over," Andrew smiled.

"Declan?" Laci looked back to her brother who also smiled.

"His exact words were, 'She wants some pineapple and anchovy pizza.' At least I think that's what he said," Andrew explained.

Laci turned to Declan, "How could you?"

"What? I was hungry," Declan said as he stepped forward and took the box of pizza from Andrew.

Andrew looked at Laci in confusion until she answered, "Declan is the only one who eats pineapple and anchovies on a pizza."

Andrew laughed and said, "Then maybe you and I should go out to eat?"

"Smooth!" Declan shouted from behind them. "Laci you should go out with him just for that line alone."

"Please forgive my immature brother," Laci said loud enough for Declan to hear.

"He's helping me spend time with you…so I don't mind," Andrew whispered.

Laci smiled and went to grab her purse. Declan whispered to her, "Hey, I'm sorry but I thought you could use a break from all this stalker crap. Relax and enjoy yourself, okay?"

Laci nodded and hugged her brother, "I'm sorry Declan but thank you for always thinking of me. I don't know what I'd do without you."

"Probably become a crazy old cat lady," Declan joked.

Twenty minutes later Laci and Andrew were each eating a burger at a local bar that doubled as a karaoke joint.

"Do you sing?" Andrew asked Laci.

"Yes…badly."

He laughed, "I was going to ask you if you wanted to sing with me onstage."

"Oh no way would I do that!" Laci balked at the idea.

"Not even for me?"

"Nope…not even for the President."

Andrew laughed and asked, "Well if I sing you a song would I get extra points?"

"Points?" Laci asked not following.

"Your brother told me you gave all your boyfriends a point system," Andrew explained.

Laci felt her face heat, "Declan told you that?"

Andrew nodded and Laci said, "He's lying! I don't do that. Why are you asking Declan for information about me anyway?"

"I didn't ask. He just offered."

"Well you should never believe him. He's always joking around."

"He is?"

Laci nodded, "Yes."

"I wish I had known that before-"

"Before what?"

"I brought you to this karaoke place. He said you'd love it," Andrew explained. "He said you loved to sing when you were upset."

"He said that?"

"Yeah, he said it's how he knew when it was that time of the month. You'd be singing all around the house."

Laci wanted to die of embarrassment. She was going to kill Declan. Andrew laughed at her expression.

"Just for that, you're going to have to sing me a song," Laci told Andrew.

"What?"

"You heard me. Sing me a song and it better be good." Laci told him.

Andrew leaned forward and whispered, "And what do I get if I sing well?"

Laci was blushing again and put her hands to her cheeks, "I'll have to think about it."

He winked at her and said, "I'll be right back."

Andrew ran up to the stage and chose a song. The patrons of the bar quieted when Andrew spoke into the microphone, "This song is for my date…I'm hoping to cheer her up today."

A few woman in the audience thought he was sweet and Laci could hear them saying, "Awww."

The beginning chords of the song began to play and Laci smiled. Andrew was singing Just the Way You Are by Bruno Mars. As he began to sing into the microphone, Laci giggled when a woman in front shouted, "Woo hoo...dat boy can sing!"

Laci watched Andrew singing on stage, and couldn't help but forget everything that had transpired earlier that day. All she could see was the handsome man serenading her with one of her favorite songs.

After he was done, the audience gave him a round of applause, some wolf whistles (by both women and men), and some people were even standing.

"My date everyone," Andrew pointed to Laci and everyone stared at her while she sat in her seat, surprised by the attention.

"Kiss! Kiss! Kiss!" a man at the bar began chanting. Before she knew it the entire crowd was chanting, "Kiss! Kiss! Kiss! Kiss!"

A lady wearing a denim dress pulled Laci to her feet and dragged her to the stage to stand by Andrew. Laci tried hiding her smile and whispered to him, "I'm not one to fall for peer pressure."

He chuckled, "Then how about you kiss me because you want to not because they're telling you to."

Laci looked up at the handsome man before her. He was grinning and he winked at her, causing her to melt. Andrew leaned forward and Laci closed her eyes when she felt his lips tenderly brush up against hers. As the kiss deepened, Laci couldn't help but think that the past few weeks had been a nightmare filled with darkness and fear...but perhaps there was a light somewhere in the middle of all that darkness. Perhaps that light was Andrew.

CHAPTER 19

"There's something different about you two," George said looking between Laci and Andrew. "I can't quite pinpoint what it is...but something's really different."

They were standing in the elevator and Andrew's eyes widened as he looked at Laci. Laci shrugged.

"Did you cut your hair?" George asked Laci.

She put a hand up to her hair self-consciously, "No."

George looked at Andrew, "Did you cut your hair?"

Andrew copied Laci and put his hand on his hair, "No."

"Hmmm....there's definitely something different," George was rubbing his chin as if he were trying to solve some perplexing problem.

The elevator dinged as it stopped at their floor and Laci and Andrew quickly exited, leaving behind George.

"I've got it!" George cried walking quickly to catch up to them, "You two...you kissed didn't you?" He whispered loudly, inadvertently bumping into Andrew who had stopped moving forward.

"What are you talking about, George?" Andrew asked.

"You sly dog, you think I didn't notice the tension between you two has changed?"

"George, let's not get started on this again. We're not kids," Laci looked around to make sure no one was listening to their ridiculous conversation.

"I wish I had gotten a picture of it," George whispered to himself.

"George!" Laci couldn't believe he was still pushing the relationship bit.

George laughed, hurt. "Well, you can't blame me for trying. You know our listeners will eat this up. Let's get couple advice from the two love doctors. Oh the bits we could do are endless."

"We aren't going to do bits. The segments we do are still going to focus on the psychology of relationships George. That should never change," Laci was about to walk away when George asked them, "How about we go out to celebrate tonight?"

"No!" they both said at the same time, remembering the lap-dancing Elsa from the last time George celebrated Andrew joining their team.

"Don't forget who set you two up. Oh, and before I forget, Laci you got this letter in the mail today," George handed her a letter and walked away from them both, disappointed that they didn't want to go out with him.

"That was close," Andrew whispered.

"Yeah," Laci nodded and placed the letter George had given to her in her purse. "I feel slightly bad. I'd feel worse but I've been through several of George's celebrations. They never end well."

"So how about you and I do something tonight?" Andrew asked her smiling.

"Sorry but I already have a date," Laci said apologetically.

"What? I thought we were…you know," Andrew was looking uncomfortable, making Laci laugh.

"Dr. Brett, how can you be so indirect? You're a relationship expert but you won't ask me to be your girlfriend?"

"Well…it's different when it's your own relationship."

Laci laughed, "Fine. I'll do it. Andrew Brett…wanna be my boyfriend?"

"You mean exclusively?"

"Definitely," Laci grinned.

Andrew pretended to have to think about it, "I don't know. I have a lot of women after me."

Laci rolled her eyes, "Spare me."

Andrew laughed and put his arm around Laci, "I'd love to be your boyfriend. Should we get couple rings or matching clothes to commemorate this wonderful day?"

Laci laughed, "Not necessary."

"So what are we going to do tonight?"

"Andrew, I'm sorry but I was serious. I really do have a date tonight."

"With who?"

Laci smirked, "My brother's best friend."

"What?"

"My brother's friend is going to install a security alarm tonight."

"Why so late? Can't he do it during the day?" Andrew asked.

Laci shook her head, "No. I asked him to install it late so that I could be there when he did it."

"Well I'll come over if it's okay with you."

Laci laughed and joked, "Can't stay away from me, can you?"

Andrew stood still for a moment and stared at Laci, "Nope. Not even for a minute."

"So I press the button and then enter my code and the alarm is activated?" Laci asked Robert, who had just finished installing the alarm.

"Right," Robert looked at Andrew who was hovering over Laci.

"That seems easy enough," Laci whispered.

"I don't know…you're pretty bad at anything technical," Declan caught a glance at Robert who was still looking at Andrew.

"Whatever Declan. This is easy," Laci slid the keypad cover down.

"Well, I should get going," Robert said, picking up his bag of supplies.

"Already? I thought you wanted to go hit up a bar or something," Declan pouted.

Robert smiled, "Sorry. I already have plans."

"With your girlfriend?" Declan asked snidely.

"Girlfriend?" Laci asked. "I thought you two just broke up."

"Correction. She dumped him but they got back together," Declan had his arms crossed and was looking at Robert in disappointment, "Don't you know the bro code man? Bros before -"

"Don't even say it Declan!" Laci cut him off.

Robert and Andrew laughed at Laci and Declan arguing with one another.

"Thank you for all your help Robert," Laci said as they walked to the door. Her cell phone rang and she excused herself.

"Dr. Cummings?" the voice on the other end asked.

"This is she. Who am I speaking with?" Laci didn't recognize the number that had populated on her caller ID.

"This is Officer Stewart. I just wanted to give you a call about Henry Meiser."

"Oh. I wasn't expecting a phone call but I appreciate it. Did you need another statement from me regarding what happened in my home the other day?"

"Was he the guy? Did he murder Marie Ann Davis?"

"No. He had an alibi. He was released early this morning. I wasn't sure if I should call you to let you know but you previously claimed someone was stalking you and after what happened at your house…I thought you should know."

"Thank you for calling me and letting me know," Laci disconnected the call and walked back to where her brother, Andrew, and Robert were standing.

"Who was it Laci? You look as pale as a ghost," Declan looked concerned.

"Henry Meiser isn't the guy," Laci whispered.

"The guy?" Robert asked.

"I told you my sister's friend was murdered. Well apparently this Meiser guy was also writing creepy lover letters to her in his diary."

"Declan!" Laci didn't want him discussing the personal life of her clients.

"Don't worry Laci. The alarm will keep intruders

out," Robert assured her.

"Thanks Robert. You've been incredibly helpful," Laci hugged him before he left.

Declan looked at Laci and Andrew and smiled, wriggling his eyebrows up and down, "So what are your plans for tonight?"

Andrew quickly grabbed Laci' purse and shoved it at her, "Let's go before we get a third wheel."

He was joking but Nichols scowled, "Not nice."

Laci opened her purse and noticed the envelope George had given her earlier. It was an egg shell color. She opened it and smiled.

"What is it?" Andrew asked.

"A wedding invitation. A listener I helped out invited me to her wedding. I guess she sent the invitation to the radio station."

"A wedding?" Declan groaned, "I feel sorry for the poor sucker that gets roped into going with you to that." He quickly walked out of the room in the event that the poor sucker would be him.

"It's a wedding for Veronica Watson and Clay Garmon. It's in a couple of weeks. Did you want to come with me?" Laci asked Andrew.

"Veronica Watson? She was your listener?"

"Yeah. She had been in an abusive relationship but finally got out of it. Now she's getting married."

"That's great," Andrew said softly.

"So do you want to go?"

"To the wedding?" Andrew asked looking behind her to see if Declan was coming back.

"No to the moon. Of course to the wedding."

"I'm sorry Laci but can I take a pass on that? I'm not a big fan of weddings."

Laci was disappointed but didn't argue with him. It

was still too early in their relationship for her to be making demands. She smiled and put the invitation back in her purse. Declan was going to be the poor sucker that went with her and that was final.

Amber stared at the picture of Laci Cummings and Andrew Brett laughing in the studio of their radio show. She scrolled down to the comments section of the website for Love Guru and frowned. It looked like a majority of the listeners were in favor of the two being a couple.

"Of course Miss Perfect is dating the perfect boyfriend."

She had typed in a rude comment the other day but Kay had made her delete it. Now she was alone and she could type whatever she wanted, "This relationship is fake. They're only pretending to date for ratings. The truth is that she's living with another man!"

She sneered at her comment. Readers wouldn't know that the other man was her brother.

Amber didn't always hate Laci. The truth was Laci was that woman that seemed to get everything easily and it bothered Amber. Laci was beautiful, confident, smart, and was able to make friends with everyone. It was tough trying to keep up with her.

When Laci had her own magazine, Amber had been happy for her. After Laci got her own talk show, Amber started to resent her a little. That feeling continued to grow each time Laci inadvertently bragged about her job. Amber would remind herself that Laci wasn't trying to brag…she was just sharing an interesting bit of information about her job. Still, it came across as bragging to Amber. None of them were married or had kids so they usually discussed work.

At one point she thought of emulating Laci and listened to her radio show religiously. The real reason she broke up with Officer Joe Bishop was because he wasn't good enough. Amber had originally thought an officer would be a boyfriend she could show off. However, she heard Laci talk to a listener on her show.

"Dating a police officer or anyone in a dangerous job is stressful and I don't envy you."

I don't envy you.

Those words were enough to cause Amber to dump Officer Bishop.

Then she started dating her new boyfriend who was starting his own small company. She never told Laci about it because it was something she secretly held over the psychologist.

I have a boyfriend and you don't.

Even Kay and Marie Ann didn't know about him. She still wasn't sure if he was good enough. Especially now that Laci was dating Dr. Andrew Brett.

She heard a knocking on the door and shouted, "Come in. It's open!"

Amber wrapped her arms around him and greeted him back, "Hey Robert."

CHAPTER 20

"One cup of chocolate chips…and two sticks of butter," Kay was reading a list of ingredients off of a recipe for chocolate chip cookies she wanted to try. "I am so not domestic." She placed the list down and reached for her cellphone. It had been a week since she heard from Judas.

"Guys are such jerks. Is it that hard to give me a call?" she was tempted to text him but didn't want to appear needy. She refused to text him first.

Kay was about to delete his number when it suddenly started ringing, "Is he psychic?"

Flashing across the screen was Judas's name. She had met Judas a few weeks back at a graveyard which was an odd place to meet a man…but she wasn't going to focus on that fact.

"Hello?"

Judas's voice came across the line, "I'm so sorry Kay. I've been swamped with work but I'm glad I caught you."

"I thought you lost my number," Kay laughed.

"No way would I ever do that. I was calling to ask if you wanted to grab some dinner."

"Tonight?"

Judas laughed, "Yeah...tonight. And tomorrow...and maybe the day after that."

"Well I haven't seen you in a while so I want to make up for lost time."

Kay smiled. She really didn't expect to hear from Judas but she was glad that he had finally called her. "Okay, I'll meet you tonight, tomorrow night, and the night after that."

Judas chuckled on the other end of the phone and that thought, "This was going to be easy."

Laci sat in front of her vanity table, straightening her hair. It had been a little over two weeks since the whole Henry and Portia Meiser incident occurred. She had begun renting an office space to see her clients and she hadn't heard a peep from her "stalker." She was beginning to relax a little.

"Laci," Declan knocked on her door.

"You're not getting out of this so just tie your tie Declan," Laci yelled at him before he could make up another reason that he couldn't' attend the wedding of Veronica Watson. She hadn't give him too much information. She hadn't even give him a choice. The conversation consisted of her telling more than asking.

"Laci, aren't you being a bit too bossy? I'm your brother...you should be making Andrew go with you. Besides, isn't it weird to be going to the wedding of a listener? What if she's not really getting married? I mean who has a morning wedding anyway? What if she's some crazy woman and this is all a trap?"

Laci looked at her brother and held back a giggle, "Declan do you know how crazy you sound right now?"

"That's what every man thinks when you make him go to a wedding. Ask Andrew."

"Andrew would not think that."

"Oh yeah? Then why isn't he coming to this wedding with you? He's your boyfriend. If I were you, I would have forced him to come. I can't believe you let him off the hook but force your younger brother to go."

"Declan I don't know if you know this or not but I hate carrying around change so keep your two cents to yourself. I want to go to this wedding and you're coming with me. I'm using my big sister card here."

Declan turned around mumbling something about tyrannical older sisters, causing Laci to laugh.

After they were both dressed they drove to the hall where the ceremony and reception were to take place.

"So what's the name of the bride?" Declan asked turning his head towards Laci.

"Declan, pay attention to the road. There's a truck coming!" Laci pointed towards a white truck that hadn't stopped at a four-way stop.

"Relax Laci, I know how to drive."

Ten minutes later, they were seated in a large hall. To the side was where the reception would take place.

"This is fancy. When you and Andrew get married, will it be in a church?" Declan asked.

Laci sighed, "Andrew and I are just dating. Marriage isn't even on the table."

"So who is the bride?" Declan asked while looking around at all of the other guests.

Declan didn't get an answer because the wedding march began to play. The audience all turned to watch the procession of bridesmaids come down the aisle and finally Veronica, dressed in a mermaid cut wedding dress. Laci didn't care for her dress but still pretended to fawn over it as was custom of the audience.

Declan had turned around to see Veronica and then quickly turned back around to face the groom. If Laci thought his behavior was strange, she didn't say so.

After the 'I do's' were said, everyone clapped as the couple strolled back down the aisle together. Declan whispered into his sister's ear, "Let's get out of here."

She turned to him and grimaced, "Declan we just got here."

"Trust me Laci. We should go."

"I'm not going anywhere Declan. I want to congratulate her."

"Fine. I'll wait in the car."

"Declan, what's the matter with you?"

"Nothing. I'm just tired of being here."

"You're my date. You can't leave me."

"I'm not your date…I'm your hostage."

Laci rolled her eyes and dragged him towards the direction of the wine bar. Declan seemed nervous and kept looking around. Laci knew men could become jittery at the thought of attending a wedding but Declan was being ridiculous. Not even fifteen minutes had passed when he asked again if they could leave.

"Declan, what is wrong with you? I've never seen you act like this," Laci asked her brother.

Declan opened his mouth to respond when another voice cut him off.

"What are you doing here?"

Laci and Declan both turned to Veronica, the bride, still dressed in her white wedding gown. She repeated her question, but was looking at Declan, "What are you doing here?"

Laci didn't understand, "Hi Veronica, this is my brother Declan. I had him come with me."

Veronica turned to Laci, "He's your brother? Is this some kind of joke? I want you both to leave now."

"What?" Laci didn't know why Veronica was becoming upset all of a sudden.

"I said leave. Now," Veronica kept her voice low but firm so that she wouldn't get the attention of her other guests.

Laci looked at Declan who appeared pale. "Fine. We'll leave. Congratulations," Laci mumbled. She and Declan left the hall but Laci still didn't understand what had just happened.

After they were back in the car, she turned to Declan, "What was that all about?"

"This is why I told you we should've left," Declan muttered.

"Declan I'm serious. Why did we just kicked out of a wedding after she took one look at you? How did she know you?"

Declan pulled onto the highway before he answered, "We used to date."

"What? When?"

"A long time ago. We dated and I cheated on her," Declan said quietly, "It's kind of embarrassing."

"You dated her? That's unbelievable."

"Yeah...hey so she was one of your listeners? Was

it because I cheated on her? She couldn't get over it?"

"Don't flatter yourself." Laci was reminded of her original letter. It was because she was dating an abusive boyfriend. She looked at Declan and couldn't believe it. Declan was playful and laid back. He never displayed any kind of aggressive behavior. Still, she found herself asking, "Exactly how long ago did you two date?"

"A long time ago," Declan said, emphasizing the word long.

Laci nodded, "It's such a small world. Who would've guessed?"

"Yeah. It's a really small world. After she dated me she dated one of my friends. I guess to pay me back since I cheated on her with one of her friends. I don't know why she'd still be angry about it. She just got married. She should be thanking me for cheating on her since it led her to today," Declan said as he continued to drive to their home.

Laci rolled her eyes at his comment. Then she asked, "So Veronica dated one of your friends?"

He nodded, "Yeah. She dated Robert but it didn't last long. I'm not sure what happened but it was like one day they were dating the next day they weren't."

"You didn't ask why they broke up?"

"No," Declan laughed, "Why would I care? I was already dating someone else. Besides, Robert moved on pretty quickly and so did she from what I hear."

"You weren't mad at Robert?"

Declan laughed, "Bros before-"

"Don't say it unless you want me to hit you Declan," Laci warned.

He shrugged his shoulders, "No I didn't mind. Anyway, it all worked out in the end didn't it? She got married and Robert is dating some chick that he really likes."

"Awww it's just my poor baby brother that hasn't gotten a new girlfriend," Laci mocked.

Declan grinned, 'It's okay sis' I'm having too much fun finding Mrs. Right."

"Yeah, so you're settling for Mrs. Right Now."

As they pulled into their driveway, Laci thought of Andrew's reaction which was a little similar to Declan finding out that he knew the bride. She wondered if Andrew also knew Veronica in some way.

"Was that why he didn't want to go?" she wondered.

"Who didn't want to go?" Declan asked.

Laci hadn't realized that she was talking out loud, "Oh nobody. I was just talking to myself." Still, Laci wondered if   Andrew had any possible relationship to Veronica.

"We've been seeing one another...pretty much every night. I'd say we're boyfriend girlfriend. Do you agree?" Judas asked while pouring her a glass of wine.

Kay blushed, "Oh...I don't know. Maybe we're just two people that enjoy each other's company?"

"And bodies?"

They both laughed and Judas leaned in to kiss her but Kay pushed him back, "Hold on. I want to change into something more...comfortable."

Judas grinned and watched as she headed to her bedroom. He slipped a small pill into her wine and watched it fizzle and disappear. When she returned, she was wearing sweatpants and an oversized T-shirt, making Judas laugh.

"Sexy," he told her.

She shrugged, "I try."

He handed her the glass of wine she had been drinking from earlier and said, "Let's make a toast."

"Okay."

"A toast to us."

Kay smiled and drank her wine until the wineglass was empty.

"Wake up Kay. Wake up," Jakes voice was disturbing her thoughts.

Kay slowly opened her eyes to find herself tied to her bed and thought, "What's happening?"

Everything was a bit blurry to her so she didn't understand what was going on. She tried speaking but couldn't. A large piece of cloth was stuffed in her mouth. She started to panic.

She heard Judas laugh and she instantly became more alert when she felt the cool barrel of a small gun pressed against her temple. Judas stood to the side, holding his phone, "I need to take a picture of this, so say cheese."

CHAPTER 21

Kay watched Judas scan his phone's photos through blurry vision. She had been bawling in fear as he took pictures of her in distress.

"I'm going to die," she thought. "I'm going to die wearing gray sweatpants and an ugly T-shirt."

It really didn't matter. She didn't want to die. She didn't understand how she missed the signs with Judas. He seemed so kind and sweet.

"So did the serial killer Ted Bundy," she thought.

Judas smiled as he looked at one of his pictures and held up the phone for her to see, "It's beautiful, isn't it? Like something out of glamour shots. Fear looks good on everyone."

Kay couldn't speak as her mouth was gagged. She could feel the tears staining her cheeks.

"Are you surprised by all this Kay?" Judas asked. When she didn't respond he became angry and pulled her hair, "Nod yes or no."

Kay quickly nodded.

"I'm not sure why. We met at a graveyard. How else

did you expect this relationship to end?" He began laughing at his question but Kay just shuddered. "Do you want to know why I'm doing this? Do you?" He sat on the bed and held the gun in one hand and his phone in the other, "It has nothing to do with you. It's too bad actually. I kind of liked you. Kind of."

Kay was watching his hand with the gun. Her body tensed each time he waved his hand around. Her wrists and legs were beginning to go numb from being tied up.

"I guess this means we're breaking up, huh? Well I want to let you know that it's not you. You're not the reason we're breaking up. It's your friend Laci."

Laci?

Kay didn't understand.

Did Judas know Laci?

"I can see by your surprised expression that you're wondering how I know Laci. I know her very well. She's the woman that ruined not one but two of my relationships. It's that show of hers…it gives her too much power over women. It's like she's brainwashing them to think I'm some kind of jealous monster. I'm not a monster Kay! I'm not!"

Kay found that hard to believe as he waved the gun in the air again. Kay saw the look of mania in his eyes and it frightened her. How could anyone have so much hate in them?

"The thing is…if I want to get her to do what I say…I have to go through someone she knows. Someone she cares about. And it's so much easier to tie down a woman than a man. So whether you like it or not, you're going to help me Kay. You're going to help me ruin her career and her life."

Dr. Laci Cummings was rummaging through her purse when she heard her phone dinging, alerting her of a message. She ignored it. A few minutes later, Andrew walked in and greeted her, "Hey Laci, are you ready for today's show?"

"Of course I'm ready. What better topic could we possibly discuss?"

"I can think of a few," Andrew said looking suggestively at her legs.

Laci chuckled, "You know I can still get the number to HR, Dr. Brett." He laughed in response and she smiled.

"So when we bring up men in abusive relationships, what stance do you want to take?" Andrew asked.

"I think we should both take the same stance...that it's an ongoing serious problem that needs more attention. Is there an alternative stance?"

Andrew smiled, "Sounds good to me. Alright, I'll see you in the studio."

Laci watched Andrew walk out of their shared office and smiled. A few minutes later, her phone dinged again. This time she picked it up.

It was a photo message. She allowed it to download and gasped. It was a picture of her friend Kay, gagged and tied up, with a gun to her temple.

The second message read, *"Do you value your friend's life? Reply yes or no."*

Laci quickly swiped her finger over the keys, *"Yes."*

Her phone dinged a second time. She read the message, *"Keep your phone with you and listen to my instructions."*

Another ding sounded from her phone.

"I'll be listening."

Laci started to panic. She wanted to call the police. It was the only choice she had. She was about to dial 911 when a new message populated on her screen.

"Call the cops and she dies."

She felt her knees buckle beneath her and she struggled to breath. He was back. Her stalker was back.

A shaky Laci sat behind the microphone she normally used when doing the show. Her phone was on silent but placed in front of her.

She heard Andrew speak, "Okay listeners. Today we're talking about abusive relationships and before you think we're covering the same old thing…I want to tell you that this time we're focusing on abused men. That's right you heard me. Abused men."

Andrew looked at Laci who was quiet. He gave her a confused look as she didn't reply and continued, "It's a well hidden secret that there are many men that are actually victims of abuse in their relationships. So tonight I'm calling out for all these men to be brave and give us a call. You will stay anonymous. We're here to help. Isn't that right Laci?"

Laci was startled at the sound of her name but she recovered quickly, "Right. We're here to listen to your side of the story."

Laci looked up to see George signaling them that there was a caller on the line. Andrew answered, "Welcome to Love Guru. We're glad you called."

"Hello my name is Judas," the caller answered.

"Judas, we don't use real names," Laci said in a low voice.

"That's right. Sorry about that. Hmmm in that case, I want the name Stitching Hurt."

Laci took a deep breath. The name Stitching Hurt sounded familiar but she couldn't remember where she had heard it before.

"It's an interesting choice but we'll go with it. Do you mind sharing your story with us, Hurt?" Andrew asked.

"The main woman in my life is very controlling. She doesn't let me have a relationship with anyone else. She always seems to sabotage it," Judas answered.

"Is this woman your girlfriend?" Andrew asked.

"Sort of. We're very much connected," Judas answered.

"Today we're talking about men who suffer from abuse. Is this what you're undergoing Hurt?" Laci asked.

She heard the caller laugh, "There are all types of abuse. There's physical but wouldn't you agree that mental abuse is just as bad...if not worse? It can leave a scar so deep that perhaps nothing can heal it. Can fill it."

"Would you feel comfortable telling us what you've been through?" Laci asked.

"Of course," Judas answered. "My woman is selfish. She only cares about herself. She always tells everyone that I'm in the wrong and makes me feel like crap. She steps on my ego."

A message silently flashed on Laci' phone, *"Tell him to get over it."*

Laci stared at the message, torn about what she

should do.

"DO IT!" a new message demanded.

Laci cleared her throat, "Umm bruises…I think that you should…get over it."

"What?" Andrew asked, surprised.

Laci steeled herself to continue on, "I said…you should get over it. Get a backbone. This woman will never respect you if you don't respect yourself. Ladies am I right?"

The caller responded, "Are you saying I'm a wimp?"

Another message flashed on her phone, *"Tell him yes."*

Andrew answered for her, "Not at all. Don't misunderstand Dr. Cummings. What she meant to say-"

"Yes," Laci interrupted. "Yes. I'm saying you're being a wimp. Not in a physical sense but emotionally. You should stand up to your girlfriend or this will be a problem that never gets resolved."

"I can't believe you just insulted me," the caller cried in indignation.

"She didn't mean it as an insult but as a way to get you to stand up for yourself. To motivate you," Andrew defended her.

"Take it how you want," Laci answered. She was angry at the situation she was being forced in. She was also scared. She looked up to see George gesturing wildly for her to be quiet. As a new message flashed on her screen, she knew it was going to be a long night.

"What were you thinking Laci? Do you know how many complaints we're going to get now because of you? We probably lost listeners because of the stunt you just pulled. What possessed you to tell a caller that he was a wimp?" George was livid.

Laci tried to seem unconcerned and shrugged, "It could've been worse. I could've said worse."

"Worse than telling a caller he was a wimp for being abused by his girlfriend? I don't think so."

"I'm sorry George," she said quietly.

"Sorry? You're sorry?" George went from being upset to sounding regretful, "Yeah so am I. Let's just hope the listeners aren't demanding your pink slip after tonight."

George walked away and Laci glanced at Andrew who was staring at her.

"Laci?"

"What is it?"

"Are you okay?" Andrew asked her.

His concern was almost enough to break her.

Almost.

"I'm fine. Listen, I have to get home. I'll see you tomorrow okay?"

She didn't wait for him to answer, she just walked away. It was probably for the best to stop their relationship before it really got started. She didn't know who this stalker was but she had a feeling that he was going to ruin a lot more than her radio show and she didn't want Andrew involved.

☐

CHAPTER 22

"Laci are you sleeping? Laci can you hear me? Laci?" a soft whisper of a voice drifted in and out of her subconscious.

A different voice, more familiar and distinct, cried out to her *"Laci! Laci please help me. Don't let me die!"*

The whispering voice returned, *"You can save her Laci. All you have to do is...kill yourself. Die Laci! Don't you care about your friend?"*

The woman's voice echoed the whisperer's question, *"Don't you care about me?"*

A low cackle filled her head followed by, *"I guess not."*

A scream shattered all around her. Laci sprang up from her bed, gasping for breath. Her sheets were damp and her body was covered in a sheen of her own sweat. She looked around her and saw that she was sitting up in her bed, alone.

She slowly got out of bed and pulled her sheets off, letting them fall to the floor. She padded to the bathroom and turned on the shower. She refused to go back to sleep covered in her own sweat.

Afterwards, she put on some Mickey Mouse pajamas and sat in front of her laptop. Since she had it cleaned for viruses, she hadn't downloaded any attachments from any e-mails.

She opened her advice column account and began skimming through the messages. It was linked to an IM account that she hardly ever used. She was about to set the notifications to show she was unavailable when a message popped up.

"Dr. Cummings? OMG are you really online this late? I have a question for you!"

Since she was up and had nothing better to do, she replied, *"It's pretty late. Why are you still up? I hope it's not a serious relationship problem."*

"I'm obsessed with your show. I wanted to know what I should do if my boyfriend is interested in other girls."

Laci smiled. This was easy territory for her and a change from having to try and solve the problem of her friend being held hostage. She still wasn't sure if she should contact the police. What if she called the cops and he killed Kay? She sighed as she typed, *"Are you sure he's interested in other girls?"*

"Yes, he's always trying to spend time with them. I don't know why if he has me. We met at a Jalisco's. I love their burritos!"

"Yes, their food is good. As far as your boyfriend, maybe he's just very social," Laci offered. She was pretty sure the person on the other end was a teen as their screen name was SchoolSux201.

"If you had a boyfriend and you couldn't trust him, what would you do?" SchoolSux201 asked.

"I'd probably talk to him about it," Laci answered with a tapping of her keyboard.

"That's easier to say than to do."

Laci smiled and typed, *"Yes. It is. I still think you should try. I'm not sure how old you are but no relationship lasts without trust."*

"Thanks Dr. Cummings. You're such a genius! <3<3"

Laci laughed and typed, *"I wouldn't say that. I've just been in enough relationships to know better."*

"I just don't want to be cheated on. I think that's the worst."

"I agree." Dr. Cummings laughed. If only her life was this simple. How happy she would be if her biggest problem was that her boyfriend cheated on her.

"Have you ever had a boy cheat on you?" SchoolSux201 asked.

"I believe it's a rite of passage for all girls. It's the only way they learn how to pick a good boyfriend."

"Wow I can't believe anyone would cheat on you. I feel like we have so much in common. We both like Jalisco's. We've both been cheated on and we both like Mickey Mouse."

A moment of silence passed before Laci took in what she just read.

"We both like Mickey Mouse."

She looked down at her Mickey Mouse pajamas and started shaking. She slammed her laptop shut, causing her to be hidden in complete darkness. She stood up and bumped into some furniture as she grabbed her phone and walked out of the room. She was breathing heavily. She was panicking. It was only 3:30 AM and she was too scared to go back to bed much less go back to her bedroom. She walked to her kitchen and grabbed a butcher knife. She carried it with her to the living room and sat down, her knees up against her stomach. In one hand she carried the knife and in the other she held her phone.

This was how Declan found his sister the next

morning. She was huddled on the sofa, eyes bloodshot, and her head drooping to one side as she was trying her best not to fall asleep.

"Laci? What's wrong with you? What are you doing?" her brother asked.

"Declan?" she was still in a sleepless stupor.

"What's wrong Laci?"

"I need you to call Robert. Now."

"Robert? Why?"

"I want him to do a sweep of the house. I think someone is spying on me again."

"Laci are you joking right now?" Declan asked.

Laci almost lost it. She began sobbing and yelling, "Do I look like I'm joking? I want him here now Declan! Now!"

"Okay…okay! I'll call him. Just calm down, alright?"

That morning Robert came over with a case of equipment. He took one look at Laci and whistled. "You're a sight for sore eyes."

"Don't lie Robert. We both know she looks like crap," Declan said.

Laci ignored him, "Robert did Declan tell you what I need done?"

"He said you think you have a bug in the house…or that someone was spying on you."

Laci nodded, "I know you probably think I'm crazy but I still want you to check. Can you do that?"

"Of course I can Laci. We'll start down here. Okay?"

Laci nodded and watched as Robert walked around the house with some small gizmo. He also searched the room for any hidden cameras. When he was done, he shook his head, "There's nothing here. Should I check upstairs?"

"Yes!" Laci stood up and led him to her bedroom,

"Check here first Robert."

Robert turned on his gadget that was supposed to pick up on any listening devices and he made a strange face.

"What is it?" Laci asked.

"Just a moment." Robert put his gizmo down and opened his case of tools. He took a chair and stood on it to reach the air conditioning vent. "Do you ever clean back here Laci?"

"No. Why?"

"Because if you did…you would've found this," Robert said removing the vent and pulling out what looked like a white orb with a camera in the middle.

Declan stepped forward and held it, "What is this?"

"It's a baby monitor," Robert answered.

"This is a baby monitor? Why is it in the vent?" Declan asked, still confused.

Laci felt her knees buckling beneath her.

"Aren't baby monitors one sided?" Declan asked.

"Do you not listen when I talk about work?" Robert asked. "This isn't just an ordinary monitor. It has a camera. This camera can move in any direction. Most importantly…if it's connected to your internet, then anyone can spy on you, talk to you, hear whatever you say. This is an easy doorway into your home."

"I don't believe this," Laci whispered to herself.

Robert looked at Declan who was slightly pale, "Guys, what's going on here? Why did you have me sweep your house? Is everything okay?"

"It's fine! Everything's fine," Laci stood back up. "Nothing is wrong. She grabbed the white baby monitor and held it in front of her, so that whoever was watching her could get her message directly, "Stop it! I don't know what your problem is but stop it! Leave me alone! Leave me alone!"

Declan and Robert were both stunned. They had never seen the cool and collected Laci become so riled up.

"Laci calm down," Declan stepped towards her but she quickly side-stepped him.

"Calm down? Me? Calm down? Don't you know that's the worst thing to say to someone that's not feeling calm Declan?" She held the monitor in her hands and threw it against the wall as hard as she could, causing it to break.

"Let's see if you keep spying on me now," Laci was panting.

Robert turned to Declan, "I don't know exactly what's going on but if this person hacked into your internet, you may want to change your Wi-Fi password."

Declan nodded as he watched Laci. She was standing still, staring at the broken pieces of the monitor.

After Robert was done searching the house, he confirmed that the only monitor found was the one in the vent.

"So where are they watching me from?" Laci asked.

"Their laptop or tablet most likely. All they needed to do was get it in there and hack into your router," Robert answered. "We should probably call the police now."

"No!" Alex cried, "No police."

"How long has this been going on?" Robert asked, startled by her outburst.

"A couple of weeks," Declan answered as Laci had shut down and wasn't speaking.

"Has she noticed anyone different hanging around?"

Robert asked.

"I don't know. She has tons of fans so it could be anyone couldn't it?"

"I'm right here boys. Don't talk about me like I don't exist," Laci said in a low monotone voice.

Robert was about to apologize when the doorbell rang.

Declan stood up to answer the door. It was a delivery from 1-800-Flowers. "I have a delivery for a Dr. Laci Cummings," the man said at the door.

Declan signed and took the delivery.

"That's different," Robert said, causing Laci to turn around and gasp. It wasn't a bouquet of flowers. It was a bouquet of fruit cut up into the shape of flowers.

Declan handed the card to Laci who read it. "They're from Andrew."

"That guy is too smooth. You love these flower fruits, right?" Declan asked his sister.

Laci nodded, "Declan. Did you tell Andrew I liked these?"

Declan seemed surprised by her question, "No. Didn't you tell him?"

Laci shrugged but she couldn't remember ever telling him that bit of information. She thought back to what Robert had just mentioned.

"Has she noticed anyone different hanging around?"

All of this stalker business began around the same time Andrew had come into her life. An uncomfortable feeling started to form in the pit of her stomach. Andrew was handsome and sweet. He wouldn't need to stalk women. They'd come to him willingly. It wasn't possible. Was it?

CHAPTER 23

"Laci, we need to call the police," Declan spoke, interrupting his sister's thoughts.

Robert nodded, "Right. I don't understand exactly what's going on but you should call the cops if someone's trying to stalk you. Is it that crazy guy from before?" Robert was referring to Henry Meiser.

Declan watched as Laci shook her head, "No. The police told me it wasn't him. He had an alibi around the time I was getting the notes and around the time Marie Ann was killed."

Robert looked at Declan, "Marie Ann is your sister's friend that you were telling me about?"

"Yeah. I told you things have been crazy around here," Declan handed Laci her cell phone which she had put down on the coffee table, "Call the cops Laci."

She reached for the phone as it began to ring.

It was Andrew.

Laci felt herself swallowing in nervousness. She looked at her brother as she clicked the green button, accepting his call.

"Hey Laci. Did you get my fruit bouquet?" Andrew asked.

Laci cleared her throat, "Yeah. I got it. Thank you."

"I had a feeling you would like it."

"It's weird that you knew I liked fruit bouquets. Was it just a guess?" Laci asked.

Laci saw her brother roll his eyes, "Laci. Tell your boyfriend you'll call him later. You have to call the cops. Now!"

"Is something wrong?" Andrew asked, as he was able to overhear Declan.

"A couple of things have come up. I'll tell you about it later," Laci remained vague.

"Laci, the cops? Screw it. I'll call them myself," Declan pulled his cellphone out of his pocket and Laci stood up.

"You're calling the cops?" Andrew asked, overhearing Declan.

"Listen. I'll tell you about it later. I have to go. Bye Andrew." Laci hung up on him before he could speak.

"Please don't tell me you're going to be stupid and not call the cops?" Declan asked, a look of disbelief on his face.

"It's not that simple Declan!" Laci ran a hand through her dark hair and groaned in frustration. She was at her breaking point and she knew it. "It's not that simple."

"How is it not simple? Someone has been spying on you! It's illegal! Someone snuck into this house and planted some stupid monitor crap in your room! For all we know it was the same guy who broke in and gave me a black eye." Declan had his hands on his hips. He turned to his friend Robert and asked, "Don't you agree with me?"

Robert remained quiet, watching the both of them. His eyebrows furrowed together as he thought aloud, "Honestly, I think your sister is an intelligent woman. If she didn't want to call the cops, there's probably a good reason." He looked at Laci, "It's probably a very scary reason."

"What?" Declan sighed. "Just spit it out Robert. What are you trying to say?"

Robert shrugged, "Fear is a great way to control someone."

Laci sat back down, pale. She lifted her hands to cover her ears.

"Laci?" Declan asked, "I know that this is all scary for you but I'm here. I'm here for you. I'll help you in any way that I can. Do you know how hard it is for me to see all this happening to you? We have to call the cops."

"He's got my friend," Laci whispered.

Both men heard her and looked at one another in surprise.

Robert spoke first, "Laci, when you say he's got your friend...what do you mean?"

Tears were slowly trailing down her cheeks, "He's got her. He threatened to kill her if I called the cops."

"Son of a-"Declan was cut off by Robert.

"Laci, we still need to call the police."

"And what if he kills her?" her voice rose in panic. "She's one of my best friends! He already killed Marie Ann. What if he kills Kay too?"

"This isn't something you can handle or negotiate. You should know that," Robert chided softly.

Laci sniffed, "I know that! You think I don't know

that?"

"Call the cops Laci. We'll be here for you," Declan stepped forward and wrapped an arm around Laci.

"You're right. Now that the monitor is found, there's no way he'll know anyway. It should be okay," Laci whispered more for her own peace of mind.

She picked up her phone and dialed the number to someone she could trust, Officer Tracy Stewart.

James Palmer wished he had finished college. If he had, maybe he would've been able to get a better job than as an assistant apartment manager. He wondered if it wasn't too late to quit and go back to school.

James stared at Seth Mathis, the manager of Olive Lake apartments, watching him scratch his armpits and other probably unclean areas.

James's fake smile was reaching its limit.

Seth led James to a golf cart. Today he was showing James how to do the monthly apartment inspections. "Every quarter, the apartments we inspect change."

"So we can just go into their apartments?" James asked.

"Of course! It's in the lease and we already gave them advance notice James. The tenants are supposed to crate their dogs if they have any inside the apartment. We should know which apartments have dogs since they have to pay a pet deposit."

"Do we ever have apartments that have pets without a deposit?" James asked.

Seth nodded, "Yeah. Some tenants think they can get one past me. I can tell when they have a pet without permission. The carpet is usually soiled and there's a certain smell the apartment gives off."

James grimaced. This job sounded horrible so far. He watched Seth rub his beefy hands together before he started the golf cart. James asked, "So today we're going to do apartment inspections to check for any major damages and for unauthorized pets?"

"You got it partner," Seth said in a country accent, making James cringe. "The first apartment we're going to is number four hundred," Seth explained as he pulled up in the golf cart to the building with a large number four on it. Seth and James walked to the apartment with the number four hundred and knocked.

No one answered the door. Seth knocked again. Still, there was no answer.

Seth looked at James, "Now the tenant may be at work, so we go in and just leave one of our notes." He held up a stack of half-sheets of paper that were attached to a clipboard he was holding. They were notices indicating that an apartment inspection had been done.

James nodded and unlocked the door as Seth instructed him to. The apartment was quiet and immaculate in its cleanliness.

"This person must've taken our notice that we were coming seriously," Seth smiled as he stepped into the kitchen, "James, you go ahead and check the bedroom. Just make sure that the blinds aren't broken or missing and that the door handles are still working."

James nodded and stepped to the bedroom door which was locked. He opened it, "Door handle works," he called out to Seth, who was inappropriately looking through the tenant's refrigerator.

James rolled his eyes and stepped into the bedroom. What he saw shocked him. A woman was tied to the bed. She was wearing sweat pants and a large T-shirt. Over her face was a large pillow. Her lack of movement and the failure of her chest to rise and fall indicated that she was no longer living.

His mouth opened, but words wouldn't come out. Pricks of fear spread down his back. James stood there in shock. He wasn't sure what he was looking at but he knew it wasn't good.

"Are you done in there James? We have to finish before noon," Seth called out. When James didn't respond, he walked into the bedroom. He stood beside James and dropped his clipboard. He pulled out his phone to call 911.

James was finally able to speak, "Seth?"

"Yeah?"

"I quit."

Officer Tracy Stewart was sitting across from Dr. Laci Cummings, fuming. "Explain to me again why you didn't report this sooner?"

"He threatened to kill her if I called the cops," Laci' eyes were bloodshot and puffy from crying.

"You received this message yesterday?"

Laci nodded.

"Has your stalker sent you any other messages?" Stewart asked.

Declan spoke up, "He sent me pictures of Laci."

"You?" Stewart asked.

Declan nodded, "Not too long ago. He left a note telling me to leave Laci alone for a night. He sent a bunch of pictures too. It scared the heck out of me."

"I want to see the note," Stewart said.

"Sorry. I tore it up," Declan grimaced. "I was angry. I still have the pictures though."

Officer Stewart looked at him suspiciously, "Fine. I want to see them. Anything you've received, I want."

"Thank you for believing me," Laci whispered.

Tracy Stewart had already called in a unit to drive by Kay's home and check on her. She was surprised to get the call from Laci and decided not to tell Officer Joe Bishop about it. He hated Laci and wasn't afraid to show his hostility. She held the pieces of the broken monitor in a plastic baggie. "You should have brought all of this to our attention sooner," she scolded.

"I tried to," Laci whispered.

"You asked us to close your case," Stewart reminded her. "I'm not going to lie Dr. Cummings. I understand that people are afraid to call the police when someone they care about is being threatened. It's a scare tactic I would never have expected you to fall for."

"I understand what you mean…but when it's affecting you personally. It's not as easy to be so detached. I feel like I'm slowly losing control of everything in my life and it terrifies me Officer Stewart. I'm wondering when I'll lose my sanity."

Officer Stewart nodded in understanding. Earlier, Laci had practically begged her to find Kay. She hadn't turned off her CB radio and the sound of the static-like voices filled the room of crimes around the town of Roswell.

"Tell me your friend's address," Stewart had a pen out and a small pad.

"It's the Olive Lake apartments across town. I don't know the exact address."

Stewart nodded as another report came in through the CB radio, "10-54 at 1515 Olive Cove. Olive Lake apartments. All available units please respond."

Laci paled, "What's a 10-54 mean?"

Stewart sighed. She didn't believe in sugar-coating things, "It means a possible dead body."

Declan ran to his sister and hugged her as she began to bawl. Meanwhile, Robert, who had been sitting in a loveseat across the room, looked at the time on his phone. He wondered what Amber was up to.

He was feeling antsy. On his desk was a framed picture of Laci leaving the radio station. The glass covering the picture was cracked and he smiled as he looked at it. By now, the body of Kay had been found, identified, and at the morgue. They wouldn't be able to trace it back to him. He had been very careful to erase any messages of him on her phone. He had never allowed her to take a picture of him and the number he used to contact her was under Laci's name.

He pulled out a photograph and giggled as he turned it over to scrawl a message for Laci. The photograph was placed in a gold envelope. He didn't lick the envelope but instead, used a damp cloth to wet the seal. He couldn't stop giggling as he thought of how

she would react when she saw his new message and whispered to the framed picture, "You ruined my life…now I'm ruining yours."
☐

CHAPTER 24

Denial, anger, bargaining, depression, and acceptance. Denial, anger, bargaining, depression, and acceptance.

The five stages of grief played like a broken record in Laci' mind.

Denial, anger, bargaining, depression, and acceptance.

She kept thinking she just needed to get through these five stages and everything would be alright.

Declan was coming towards her with a bottle of water, "Laci?"

She looked up at him with watery bloodshot eyes.

"It's been almost twenty-four hours since you heard about your friend and you haven't moved from the couch. I have an appointment for one of my designs. Are you going to be okay here alone? Should I call Andrew?"

"No!" Laci shouldn't have answered so adamantly because it caused Declan to give her a strange look.

"I don't want to leave you alone. Is there anyone I can call to stay with you?"

She shook her head. Yesterday had been horrific. It

had been confirmed that Kay was found dead in her apartment. She had been suffocated. Laci didn't move, didn't eat, and didn't sleep. Declan slept in the loveseat across from her so that he could keep an eye on her.

"I don't want to leave you alone. It's not safe Laci," Declan was wearing a suit jacket.

"Are you going on an interview Declan? I thought you only did freelance?" Her question surprised him since it was so out of the blue. He still answered it.

"No Laci. It's not an interview. I'm having a meeting about one of the ads I created for a local clean-up campaign. Apparently they thought something was wrong with the logo I created and they want to discuss it."

"They couldn't discuss it over the phone?"

"I asked and they said the guy in charge wanted to meet face to face. I don't know why. Some of these suits have no vision whatsoever."

Laci smiled, trying to push back her guilt regarding Kay, "You're so artistic. I bet your real parents were artists."

Declan grimaced, "It doesn't matter what they were. They gave me up for adoption."

"Yeah, I bet they were artists. Do you know what I used to think my parents were?" Laci asked ignoring his previous statement.

Declan thought the conversation was strange but he went along with it since it made his sister stop crying, "No, what?"

"Astronauts."

Declan gave a grin, "Yeah. That's interesting because I used to think you were an alien."

Laci didn't give him a reaction like she normally

would have and Declan sighed, "You know…I can reschedule my meeting. I think I need to stay here with you."

"No. You should go. I'll be fine. I'll call a friend over."

"Are you sure?" Declan asked.

"Yeah. I'm positive. Please go before I start to feel upset that you're treating me like an invalid," Laci picked up her phone and dialed Amber's number.

Amber picked up and her hello was filled with sniffles and sobs.

"Can you come over?" Laci asked her friend.

"Sure I need to talk to you anyway," Amber answered and they both disconnected the call.

Declan watched his sister and sighed, "I'm not going to be able to wait for your friend. Make sure you lock the door, okay?"

"I will. Stop worrying," Laci stood up and walked with her brother to the door.

"Who's coming over? Is it Andrew?" Declan asked, glancing at his watch.

"No it's Amber. I don't think you've ever met her."

Declan laughed, "I guess I haven't. Her name sounds familiar though."

Laci shrugged, "Hurry up and make some money bro. I want you to buy me something good to eat before you come home."

"McDonalds?" Declan smiled.

"Gross," Laci muttered.

"Okay, how about Popeyes?"

Laci rolled her eyes, "That's my brother…the big spender."

Declan pulled his sister into a hug and whispered, "I'm sorry Laci. I know this is hard on you. I wish I could help you but we're going to get past this okay?"

She nodded, a fresh batch of tears forming. "Okay...okay. I'm backing away before I cry all over you."

Declan was walking out the door when Laci called out to him, "Hey Declan..."

He turned back around, "What's wrong?"

"Nothing...just don't forget."

"Forget what?"

"Your promise to me."

"Promise?" Declan didn't understand what she was talking about.

"Your promise not to leave me, remember?"

A faint memory of Laci telling him of Marie Ann's brother being sad that his sister died came to mind. Laci was asking him not to die on her too. He gave her a big smile and waved, "Come on sis' you know I'd never leave you. Not unless a supermodel asked me to."

He laughed and walked away, getting into his truck. Laci watched him drive away and a sadness filled her. She was afraid that she would be left alone soon. Both Marie Ann and Kay had been killed. What if something happened to Declan? She didn't know what she would do.

Twenty minutes later, Amber was ringing Laci' doorbell.

"Amber," Laci tried to hug her but Amber didn't return the embrace. "How are you holding up?"

Amber's nose was red from crying and her eyes were a pink color. "Laci we need to talk."

They sat on the sofa and Amber continued, "The police talked to Kay's parents."

"Did they get any news on who did this?"

Amber shook her head, "No, but they know why it was done."

Apprehension filled Laci, "What do you mean?"

Amber shook her head in disgust, "You know exactly what I mean Laci. Why didn't you tell us?"

Laci opened her mouth but no words could come out.

"Here you are…the supposed smart one from our group and you couldn't even tell us that someone was targeting your friends? Wasn't Marie Ann's death enough? Kay's dead and now your psycho stalker is probably going to come after me!"

"Why are you acting like this is my fault?" Laci stood up and took a step away from Amber, wanting distance between them.

"How is it not your fault? A guy is after you and you didn't tell us! Then he started coming after your friends! Detective Bishop told us everything! How could you Laci?"

"I…I don't know. I'm sorry. I'm so sorry," Laci was crying again, something she didn't think was possible.

"Sorry? Is that all you can say? Well I'm sorry Laci but that doesn't cut it. Do you know how devastated Kay's parents are? When I think about Marie Ann's brother, Jacob, it makes me sick. He was so broken up over his sister's death."

"Are you trying to make me feel worse? It started off with pictures Amber. Just random pictures taken from across a room. It could've been anyone! What was I supposed to tell you guys? Hey there might be someone watching you so be careful! I didn't know what to do! He said he would kill her if I went to the cops" Laci defended herself but the words felt bitter in her mouth.

"Yeah well it looks like he killed her anyway, didn't he?" Amber crossed her arms and stood up, "Listen, I didn't want to stay long. I just wanted to tell you that Kay's family doesn't want you at the funeral."

"What?" Laci was speechless.

"You're a psychologist, you should understand that it's probably hard for them to look at you when it's your fault their daughter is dead."

Amber straightened her purse and walked past Laci as if she wasn't there. After she left, Laci sat on her sofa and cried.

Laci looked at her phone and wondered where Declan was. He still hadn't come home and several hours had already passed. She was still feeling raw and frazzled from her conversation with Amber.

The doorbell rang and she hurried to the door and answered it to see that it was Andrew.

"Hi Laci."

"Andrew, what are you doing here?"

"Your brother called me. He said you needed a shoulder to cry on. I'm sorry about your friend."

Laci wondered why Declan would call Andrew after she told him not to. "It's been a bad couple of weeks."

They were standing awkwardly at her door when he asked, "May I come in?"

Laci just stared at him as if she didn't understand until he laughed. Then she excused herself and let him in, "You really didn't have to stop by."

"Of course I did. I wanted to make sure you're

holding up okay."

"I'm fine."

"Riiight," Andrew tried to hug her but she brushed him off.

"Laci, did I do something?"

"What do you mean?"

Andrew put his hands in his pockets, "I just feel like you've been brushing me off lately and I don't understand why."

"I haven't been brushing you off," she said knowing it was a lie.

"You don't think you have?" he asked.

"No," her voice came out at a higher pitch than normal, indicating it was a lie.

Andrew laughed, "I call BS."

"What?"

"You heard me. I call BS. You've been avoiding me and I want to know why. I thought we had a great date and that you liked me."

"Andrew," Laci didn't know how to explain what was going on.

"Be honest with me Laci. We both know a relationship never works without honesty."

"Fine, you want me to be honest?"

Andrew nodded, "Yes!"

"You asked for it. The truth is that I'm scared Andrew. Do you hear me? I'm scared!"

"Of being in a relationship?" Andrew asked, surprised.

"No. Of YOU!"

"Me?" Andrew didn't know how to respond to that, "I don't understand. What did I ever do?"

"Someone has been sending me notes, pictures, crazy texts. Threatening me. Someone has been doing all that and it all started about the same time you showed up Andrew! There's something fishy about you and your too good to be true act."

Andrew was quiet for a moment. He just stared at her in disbelief.

"Well aren't you going to deny it?" Laci yelled.

Andrew let out a low chuckle and Laci took a step back.

"You're right," he whispered.

"What?" Laci had yelled at Andrew because she was frustrated but she didn't expect him to agree with her.

"I've been pretending to be better than I am. I've lied to you," Andrew looked up at Laci, "Shall I explain?"

She simply nodded, taking another step back.

"I only took this job...moved to Atlanta...all of it. I did it because of you," Andrew sat down on her sofa and placed his head in his hands.

"What are you talking about?"

"I knew who you were before I moved to Atlanta. One of my clients listened to your radio show. She used to talk to me about you so I looked you up."

Laci wasn't quite following him, "You Googled me?"

"You really know how to make a guy sound like such a loser...but yes. I Googled you. I did my research and when I saw that Modern Self was looking for and Editor, I knew that was my chance to be able to get close to you.

Laci took another step back.

"Laci," Andrew continued, "Do you believe in love at first sight?"

"No. I only believe in lust at first sight."

Andrew laughed, "Me either. At least I didn't. I

don't know…maybe I still don't. The point is I purposely took this job when they offered it to me because of you."

"Why are you telling me this?" Laci asked.

"Because I want you to know that if I seem too good to be true it's because I am! I'm trying my best to impress you; to show you what I have to offer a woman. What I have to offer you."

Laci still didn't respond.

"I don't know anything about notes, texts, or threats. I have nothing to do with that."

"Why should I believe you?" Laci asked.

Laci shook her head. She didn't know what to believe. She wanted to believe Andrew but something was holding her back. Just then her phone dinged. It was a message from a familiar number she dreaded to hear form.

She slid her finger across the home screen and looked at the message. It was a picture taken from across a restaurant. It was of her brother, Declan.

☐

CHAPTER 25

"Declan?" Laci was starting to feel dizzy, "No. This isn't real."

"Laci are you okay? What's going on?" Andrew stepped forward and looked over her shoulder at the picture of her brother on her phone.

"I have to call Declan."

Laci quickly called Declan and begged him to pick up the phone, "Come on Declan pick up...pick up...pick up."

"This is Declan. You know what to do."

Laci could feel the panic rising within her when her brother's voicemail message played. She decided to leave a message, "Declan where are you? Call me back now!"

She dialed the same number again only to hear, "This is Declan. You know what to do."

"Declan this is the second message I'm leaving you! Where are you? Call me now!"

She was about to dial his number again when Andrew grabbed her shoulder, "Laci what's going on?"

She shrugged off his hand and dialed a third time. Her message this time was of her trying not to cry in fear, "Declan...I'm begging you please call me."

"Is Declan okay?" Andrew asked.

"I don't know. I don't know. I'm going to call the police. I can't lose him too," her words were strung together and Andrew was having a hard time keeping up.

Laci was about to dial 911 when the front door opened and in walked Declan.

"Declan!" Laci ran to her brother and had him in a tight hug.

"Whoa sis' I'm glad to see you too but can you let go a little? I can barely breathe," Declan laughed trying to extract himself from his sister's bear hug.

"Why didn't you pick up your phone? I've been calling you nonstop?"

"You were? I'm sorry. I must've forgotten to take it off silent mode after my meeting," Declan said, pulling his phone out of his pocket. "Three missed calls and three messages. You really were blowing up my phone."

"Declan he's coming for you."

"Who's coming for me?"

"The man that murdered my friend," Laci whispered.

"What? Why are you saying that Laci?"

Laci pulled out her phone and showed him a picture. He looked at Andrew who was staring at the two of them curiously. Declan gave a nervous laugh, "It's...it's fine Laci. He's probably just trying to scare you."

"Well he is. I don't want anything to happen to you

too Declan."

"I'm not sure I'm following everything that's going on but if you feel threatened you should call the police Laci," Andrew stepped suggested.

Twenty minutes later, Officers Joe Bishop and Tracy Stewart were at her house.

"Is this the text?" Stewart asked.

"Yes."

"Don't worry Dr. Cummings. Technology is pretty advanced these days and we can detect which cell tower was used when the message was sent."

"Will that matter?" Andrew asked getting everyone to stare at him. "Well...it was clearly taken wherever Declan was at."

"If the phone is on maybe we still trace a signal."

"Why don't you change your number in the meantime?" Officer Bishop sighed, his hands in his pockets.

"Why don't you shut the -"

"Declan," Laci stopped him from finishing his sentence.

Officer Bishop smirked.

"I guess you're happy you got to see Amber," Laci said directly to Officer Bishop.

"What was that?" Bishop caught a quick glimpse of his partner Tracy who rolled her eyes.

"I talked to Amber. You know, your ex-girlfriend. She said you told her all about Kay's death and how it was my fault. As I said, I bet you were glad to have spoken with her. I'm sad to say that being the messenger is not the equivalent to being a knight in shining armor to a woman. If anything you're now someone she may associate with the death of her friend."

"What the heck are you talking about?" Bishop practically spit in his anger.

Declan laughed, "What she's saying is that you don't have a chance in heck with this Amber chick."

"No one asked you," Bishop sneered.

"Regardless of your personal feelings for me, your job is to serve and protect Officer Bishop. I would suggest you do so without spreading malicious gossip," Laci lifted her chin when she spoke.

"Malicious gossip?" Bishop scoffed. "How is it malicious when it's the truth? There's someone after you and he's targeting your friends and even your brother. You don't feel the slightest bit guilty?"

She did, but she wouldn't admit it. Especially not to someone like Officer Joe Bishop, "Why should I feel guilty? I'm not murdering anyone. I'm concerned and I care. These are people that I love. Why should I feel guilty? I can't control the actions of a madman."

"That's right sis' you can't control what this guy is doing. None of it is your fault," Declan draped an arm around his sister's shoulders.

Officer Bishop smiled, "I wonder if he'll think the same once this guy comes after him."

"That's enough!" Stewart said stepping in between her partner and the Cummings. She turned to Laci and apologized, "Listen I'm sorry but we should get going. We have all the information we need. I'll send some patrol cars to drive around the area."

As they were leaving, she noticed the electronic key pad, "You have an alarm?"

"Yes we just had it installed," Laci answered.

"Good. They're a great preventative measure. Keep in touch Dr. Cummings."

"Thank you Officer Stewart."

After they had left Declan cleared his throat, "Well it's been a long day. I think I'm going to hit the sack."

"Declan. Don't you want to talk about all this? Aren't you worried?" Laci asked her brother.

"Laci I love you but I don't want to talk about it. I just want to rest. I'll see you in the morning." Declan walked upstairs to his bedroom without looking back.

"He's scared," Laci whispered.

"So am I," Andrew answered, startling her. She had forgotten he was there. "I'm scared for you. Why didn't you tell me sooner what was going on?"

"How could I? Someone has been sending me texts, notes, and targeting my friends. It's been horrible," Laci said as she sat down on the sofa.

"Tell me about it," Andrew urged her.

She didn't need much prodding. Before she knew it, she had given the entire story to Andrew who was now pondering the situation.

"Laci why do you think he's targeting you?"

She shrugged, "Honestly I think he's angry with me. He doesn't seem to be obsessed in a way that would make me think he has feelings for me other than hostility. To come after my friends and now Declan makes me think he wants me to suffer. To be all alone."

"Then the suspect list could be huge."

"How so?"

"What if this is someone that's upset because you caused their relationship to deteriorate?"

"That's ridiculous! Why would someone try to kill me because I caused a relationship to fail?"

"People have killed for less. Besides, what if this person was already mentally unstable? You might have been the last straw that broke the camel's back so to speak."

"I don't know what to do anymore. If something happens to Declan...then I'll be all alone."

"Not true," Andrew whispered.

"What?"

"You won't be all alone. I'm here for you Laci. And don't worry. Declan seems like he can take care of himself."

"Are you kidding? He pretends to be tough but he's very sensitive. When we were younger, I once caught him crying because he accidentally pulled the wings off of a butterfly."

Andrew laughed, "Why would he do that?"

"He thought it would turn back into a caterpillar. He was so devastated when he found out. Besides, Declan works out and all...but when that guy broke into our house, he got his ass kicked."

"Someone broke into your house? You didn't tell me that just now."

"It feels like nothing compared to everything else that's been going on but yeah. It's one of the reasons we had the alarm installed."

"I'm sorry you've been going through all this Laci."

"I feel bad for my friends and their families. My friend Amber won't even speak to me anymore. She's so upset."

Andrew was sitting next to Laci and hugged her when she began crying, "I feel like I'm slowly losing control over everything and I'm scared Andrew. What's next? What's he going to take next?"

Andrew patted her back and tried to soothe her.

"I wish I had an easy solution for you Laci. Instead, just know that I'm here for you. I got your back."

Laci let herself soak in his comfort but she still

dreaded what the next day had in store for her.

"Are you sure you don't have to go anywhere?" Laci asked her brother Declan.

"Yes, I'm sure. Are you sure you weren't a prison warden in a past life?"

"If it'll help keep you safe, then I'm glad if I was."

"Spare me. Laci go to work already. I have some Karate Kid to watch. I need to brush up on my fighting skills."

Laci smiled and gave Declan a hug, "I love you brother."

"Yeah...yeah...I love you too sis'. Now hurry up and go to work."

Laci turned on the alarm and walked outside. She walked to her car and saw a gold note attached to her windshield. She stopped and looked around. She didn't see anyone. She walked forward and picked up the note.

In the envelope was a picture of her, dressed in her undergarments. It was an old picture, before the baby monitor had been found in her room. She remembered the day she last wore her sports bra and she hated to admit it but some very unflattering underwear. She sighed, "So he's letting me know he has pictures of me in my underwear. Big deal Laci. Don't be bothered by this. It's the same as if you were in a swimsuit."

She got in her car and drove to work. As she walked in, she waved at Oliver who simply nodded and blushed when he saw her.

"That's weird," she muttered.

Laci started to get an uneasy feeling when she noticed people around the office staring at her strangely.

"Laci!" she turned around to see George down the hall. "In my office now!"

Laci followed him into his office, "What's going on George?"

"Explain this," he held his cell phone up to her and she saw it. The picture of her in her underwear.

"Where? How? I don't...how did you get that?" Laci could feel herself getting hot with embarrassment.

"I was going to ask you why you sent it to everyone."

"What? I didn't send anything George!"

"I didn't think you did Laci but almost everyone in the building got this text message of you in your underwear. Not even good underwear Laci!"

She couldn't laugh at his attempt to joke about it. She felt like her world was caving in on her. The door suddenly opened and in walked Andrew, "Laci are you okay?"

"Who asked you to come in here?" George slammed his hand on the desk, "I'm trying to sort this out."

Andrew ignored George, "Laci, how are you feeling?"

"This isn't real. It can't be real," Laci whispered to him.

Another male voice that she recognized came from the door, "Oh it's real alright."

George stood up, "Officer Bishop. Did you find out who the sender was?"

Laci could hear him smirking, "It's the same phone number that's been sending messages to Dr.

Cummings. The same phone number that's registered under her name."

"This is ludicrous! She would never send compromising pictures of herself to anyone! Besides, she probably doesn't even have everyone's cell numbers," Andrew had a hand on one of her shoulders as he stood behind her.

"A staff directory has everyone's contact information, doesn't it?" Bishop asked George who nodded.

Officer Stewart walked in and stopped the conversation, "We're still trying to find out who the true owner of the cell phone is. Please advise your employer to advise the building employees that the message was not sent by Dr. Cummings."

A few minutes later, the officers left.

"This is a mess Laci. Just a mess," George was sitting behind his desk, tapping his fingers against the wood.

"George, I didn't send that message," Laci said feeling numb.

"I know you didn't Laci but until everything blows over, I've been given directions to put you on leave."

"What?" Andrew looked at Laci who seemed resigned, "Then who will do the show with me?"

"No one. You'll do it on your own. We may get guest hosts. All of this has to blow over. We don't know who but some of the workers have posted your picture on the internet already Laci. The message boards are blowing up. Everyone's making a big deal about it. Even the janitors are upset. They wanted to know why you were wearing granny panties. The big boss is asking for your resignation. I convinced him to put you on leave until we can figure things out."

"What if I refuse to do the show without Laci?" Andrew asked.

"You're on contract Dr. Brett. You'll only be hurting yourself."

"No," Laci shook her head, "Andrew you have to continue. Things will get cleared up and I'll be back."

"Laci-"

"No! I'm so sick of this right now. I don't know why he sent those pictures. It doesn't matter. I have bigger problems to deal with so maybe this is a good thing."

Andrew tried to stop her from walking out of the office but couldn't. She walked to the parking lot where Eric was doing his rounds.

"Hi Dr. Cummings. How are things?" the old security guard asked.

"They've been better." Laci wondered if Eric had also seen the picture of her in her underwear.

"I'm sorry to hear that. Did you and your boyfriend fight?"

Laci laughed, "No. I think I'm going to take some time off so I'll see you in a few weeks, okay?"

"That's good Dr. Cummings. You take some time for yourself. You deserve it."

Laci waved goodbye to Eric and got in her car. Instead of driving to her home, she found herself going to the cemetery.

She passed what seemed like endless graves until she stopped in front of two that she hadn't visited in a long while.

"I'm sorry I'm coming empty handed. I just wanted to stop by and say I miss you guys and I really wish you were here. You two were the best parents I could ever dream of and I'm so grateful that you adopted me. I love you both so much." Laci was sitting on the ground in front of the graves of her parents, bawling. "Dad, you used to always give me such good advice. Mom, you always listened to me talk about boys and work. I need you guys. I really need you guys right now. I don't know what to do. I'm sure you're watching over me and Declan but if you can...please just watch over Declan. I don't want anything to happen to him. Especially not because of me. Please."

As Laci wept, a solitary figure in the distance watched, smiling.

☐

CHAPTER 26

Amber was watching Robert inhale some Doritos while typing on his laptop. He said he was designing a new security system. She didn't understand how he could still be working. Amber never remembered him working like this in the past. They had dated after she broke up with Joe Bishop. Robert was fun and a few years younger than her. They fought a lot but that was probably because they were so much alike. He was handsome and successful but he was very immature. He was no Dr. Andrew Brett, that's for sure.

"This summer's gonna hurt like a-," Robert was chanting under his breath.

"Robert," Amber called out to him.

He didn't respond. Instead he kept chanting, "This summer's gonna hurt like a-."

"Robert!" Amber said in a sharper voice, almost yelling.

"What's wrong, babe?" Robert pulled himself away from his laptop and glanced at Amber who was scowling.

"I've been trying to think and I can't because you keep mumbling."

Robert chuckled, "I'm sorry. I didn't realize I was doing it."

"Well stop. It's annoying."

Robert shook his head, "I know you're upset because your friend passed away but you need to watch the attitude."

Amber frowned, "She didn't pass away Robert. She was murdered. Killed! How can you be so insensitive?"

Robert shrugged, "I didn't know her. Besides, I offered to go with you to the funeral tomorrow but you said no. What else do you want from me?"

"I've told you what I wanted."

Robert rolled his eyes, "Amber, you're older than me but you need to grow up."

"Me? I need to grow up? What's that supposed to mean?"

Robert sighed, "I'm tired of playing these games with you."

"What games?" Amber asked.

"You know what games. You need to stop being such a downer all the time."

"If I'm such a downer, why did you ask me to go out with you again? Didn't you break up with another girl to date me again? We were apart for three months. Why ask me out again?"

Robert shut off his laptop, "Honestly, I'm asking myself the same thing."

"What did you say?" Amber asked, shocked.

"You heard me. I'm sick and tired of you always nagging at me. I can't even hum to myself or you get all bent out of shape. You still won't let me introduce you to my friends. You're always putting me down. I don't get it. If you're so ashamed of me then why go out with me?"

Amber was breathing heavily, "Robert, I'm going through a tough time right now."

"Yeah? Name someone who isn't."

Amber took a step back, Robert had never gotten upset with her before. "Why are you being a jerk to me right now?"

"I'm not being a jerk Amber. I just want an answer. Are you ashamed of me?"

Amber took a second too long to answer. Robert cursed under his breath, "You know what I don't understand Amber?" He didn't wait for her to respond, "You act like I'm not good enough for you but the truth is, you're not all that."

"Excuse me?" she said, offended.

"Did I stutter? You're not that great a catch. You're older than me. I make more money than you. Even my friend Declan' sister, Laci, is better looking than you."

It was a direct hit, and Robert knew it. He knew how Amber was secretly jealous of Laci Cummings.

"I'm way prettier than her!" Amber shouted.

Robert shrugged, "Maybe in your eyes."

Amber was sputtering in anger.

"I never understood why you didn't want to meet my best friend Declan. You and I dated for four months, broke up for three, and even now you still don't want to meet him. The only thing I can think of is that you're embarrassed."

"Get out!"

"This is my apartment too. You get out!" Robert yelled at her.

Amber ran towards him and tried shoving him out the door. He held his ground, making it difficult for her. She wouldn't be able to open the door and push him out. Amber threw her hands up and attempted to scratch his face. Robert cursed and pushed her up against a wall, holding her arms above her head, "What the heck's the matter with you?"

"Let go of me!"

"You need to calm down," Robert muttered.

"Let me go!" she shouted, trying to kick her leg up to hit him in the groin. Robert threw his weight against her and said in a deep voice, "I'll leave, but I'm getting my stuff first. If I were you, I wouldn't piss me off anymore right now."

Amber was frozen in fear and anger. She wasn't afraid of Robert but this was the angriest she had ever seen him. She rubbed her wrists where he had held her and whispered, "Hurry up. Get your stuff and get out Robert."

He called her a few curse words as he gathered some clothes in an overnight bag. His parting words to her were the same ones he gave to her the last time, "You'll regret this."

Laci was making some hot cocoa and her brother Declan was standing next to her holding a bag of tiny marshmallows.

"Remind me again why we're making hot cocoa when it's hot outside?" Declan asked.

"Because it's delicious."

"Does your boyfriend know what a weirdo you are?"

Declan asked.

"He's not my boyfriend," Laci said softly.

"Really? You could've fooled me. He comes over all the time now," Declan said while eating a handful of marshmallows.

Laci slapped his hand, "Stop or we won't have any for the cocoa!"

"Marshmallow Nazi!" Declan cried after she took the bag away.

"Before I was adopted, we used to make hot cocoa in my foster home. I used to love drinking it. Even in hot weather, I'd drink it," Laci smiled.

Declan nodded, "Yeah yeah...I've heard this story before Laci."

"So rude," she laughed.

"You're lucky though. You had a good foster home and mom and dad adopted you."

"They adopted you too Declan," Laci reminded him.

He gave a thin smile, "Yeah but I still had to see some rough parts of life before they adopted me."

Laci pulled out two mugs and placed them on the counter. She stayed quiet to let Declan continue talking. It was very rare for him to discuss his life before the adoption. Laci had only really known him as her obnoxious but lovable little brother. She couldn't imagine him suffering as a young child. The thought made her heart ache.

When he didn't continue, she asked, "What was it like Declan?"

He started outlining the rim of one of the mugs with a finger, "I don't know."

"I only ask because mom and dad never really told me and you never told me. It's weird to think there's this entire chunk of your life that I don't know about.

I'm your sister. I should know everything about you."

Declan smirked, "Is that so?"

"Yes. No secrets between siblings."

Declan shook his head, "I don't think so Laci."

"Declan you're an adult now. It's okay to talk to me about it."

"I thought psychologists weren't supposed to be pushy about getting people to open up," Declan jested.

"I'm not talking to you as a psychologist. I'm talking to you as a sister. A big sister that's tired of not knowing everything about you."

"I think it's best that you don't know Laci."

"Really? Do you mean that?" Laci asked, a little hurt.

Declan sighed, "Oh and she's pulling the big sister puppy eyes card on me."

"No I'm not. I'm just surprised. You know everything about me."

Declan shook his head, "No I don't and honestly, I find it hard to believe that you don't know everything about my biological parents."

Laci turned away, "I know some stuff."

"Like what?"

Laci cleared her throat and began pouring the cocoa into one of the mugs, "That your parents were addicted to drugs."

"True, and what else?" Declan knew his sister well enough to know that she always knew more than she let on.

"That they were arrested and put in jail," she mumbled.

"And what else?"

"That there were allegations of abuse."

She wasn't facing him, but she could hear him

inhaling a gasp.

"How did you know all that Laci?"

"A couple of years ago, I looked into some old records of mom and dad and then followed up with police reports."

"All that just to find out about my childhood?" Declan mocked.

"You're my brother Declan. Of course I did that. I wanted to know more about you."

"Why?"

"Why not?" she asked.

Declan rubbed a hand over his face, "Laci, I'm an adult. I know you mean well but sometimes you treat me like a kid and it really bothers me."

Laci knew she went overboard sometimes, "I'm sorry Declan. I shouldn't have snooped. It's nothing to be ashamed of though."

"I know that!" Declan raised his voice more than he intended to. There was a moment of awkward silence. "I'm sorry Laci. It's just not something I ever wanted to talk about."

"I understand Declan. It must be tough to have been exposed to that."

"Laci, I know you're a shrink and all that but could you spare me the understanding BS. You have no idea what I went through."

"Of course I don't. You won't tell me."

Declan cursed, "You want to know? Fine! I was raised by the two most selfish people I know. They didn't care about me one bit. All they cared about was their next fix. If I bugged them and told them I was hungry, I'd get a whipping. And not with a hand or even a sandal Laci. They'd beat me with whatever was close to them. You ever been spanked with a bottle of beer before, Laci? It hurts like heck."

Laci was shocked but Declan continued, "Still, being bruised by a bottle was nothing compared to when they made me get in a bath full of water and hit me Laci. I don't know if you know this, but the water makes it hurt more."

Laci could feel tears forcing themselves out of her eyes as she watched her brother's face crumple in the sadness of his memories. "I hated them Laci! I really hated them. I was glad when the cops busted them for drugs. I never wanted to see them again. All they ever taught me was pain. The ins and outs of it. I know it well. I practically have a doctorates in it. You treat me like I'm some kind of kid and it bugs the heck out of me Laci because I haven't been a kid since I was old enough to walk."

Laci heard him take a deep breath, "I'm sorry Declan."

He raised his head and looked at her, "For what? It wasn't you that made me go hungry or kneel on broken beer bottles because I asked for a cake on my seventh birthday."

Laci wanted to hug Declan but she knew if she did, he would reject her affection. Instead she said, "It must have been very different coming from that world to being adopted here. Mom and dad were amazing and loving."

Declan gave a bitter laugh, "Different? Try alien. I used to wonder when they were going to show their true colors. It took me two years to finally trust them."

Laci nodded quietly, "Declan?"

"What?"

"I love you. You know that right?"

Declan nodded, "I know that Laci. Deep in my heart I know it. I know I joke around a lot Laci but please don't ask about my past anymore. It's not something I like to think about."

"I understand, Declan."

"Would you stop saying that? You don't understand Laci. You could have a million psychology degrees but unless you've lived through what I've been through, No amount of empathy is going to make you understand. I'm scarred for life! Can you get that through your head?" Declan took a deep breath and cursed. "I'm sorry Laci. I'm sorry."

Laci could see the tears he was trying to wipe away, "It's okay. I know that was difficult for you but you shared it anyway. Thank you Declan."

He didn't respond so she grabbed his mug and poured some cocoa in it. She then put a small mountain of marshmallows in his cocoa. "Cheer up brother. I'm here for you."

Declan was about to speak when the doorbell rang.

"Was your boyfriend coming by?" Declan asked, his voice gruff with left-over emotion.

"No," Laci murmured.

"Ah ha! You didn't deny it so you admit he's your boyfriend!" Declan was trying to lighten the atmosphere and Laci went along with it.

She laughed, "I plead the fifth."

"You can't plead the fifth!" Nichols cried.

Laci stuck her tongue at him and replied, "Says who?"

She walked over to the front door and opened it. Outside was not one but two handsome men. "Andrew! Robert!" Laci said in surprise.

Declan walked up from behind and greeted his

friend. They all stared down at the overnight bag, "What's going on Robert?"

"My girlfriend and I broke up again. Do you mind if I spend a few nights here?"

Declan looked at Laci who gave a slight smile, "Not at all. Mi casa es su casa."

"Thanks guys," Robert stepped forward and followed Declan to the living room.

Andrew waited in the doorway, "How are you doing?"

"I'm holding up," Laci answered.

"Your eyes are all red. Have you been crying?" Andrew asked.

Laci nodded, "Yes but not for the reason you're thinking."

"What reason am I thinking?" Andrew asked playfully.

"That I'm crying because I lost another friend."

"Actually," Andrew corrected her, "I was thinking your eyes were red because of allergies."

Laci genuinely laughed and allowed him to come in. Neither of them noticed Declan and Robert, quietly watching them from the kitchen. Both were wearing a frown.

☐

CHAPTER 27

"Do you mind getting a room?" Declan yelled from the kitchen. Robert chuckled as his best friend scowled at Andrew and Laci, "It's one thing to date my sister outside but in this home...I don't want to see it."

"Declan!" Laci cried, embarrassed.

"What? He's rich. He should be able to take you to some fancy hotel to paw you."

Andrew laughed, "It sounds like someone is jealous."

Declan pretended to pout, "Maybe I am."

"Fine," Robert interjected, "I'll hug you." He reached for Declan and grabbed him in a bear hug.

Declan struggled to free himself as Laci and Andrew laughed.

"I love you Declan," Robert said in a high-pitched voice.

"Dang Robert. You'll never keep a girl if you're this clingy," Declan joked as he pushed his friend away.

Robert backed away and said in a monotone voice,

"That was cold-hearted Declan."

"He's just joking Robert," Laci said stepping towards them.

"Yeah I'm just joking. We know the reason you and your girlfriend fought was because you probably cheated," Declan mumbled.

"Declan!" Laci couldn't believe her brother was joking when Robert was probably feeling hurt right now.

"What Laci? Some women just don't understand that you have to hate the other woman not the game."

"You did not just say that," Laci told her brother. She looked up to the ceiling, "Please tell me my brother did not just say that."

"He said it," Andrew laughed.

Declan winked at her and Robert actually started laughing, "I did not cheat on my girlfriend. We just realized we weren't mean to be."

"I'm sorry Robert," Laci said. "There are worst things that could be happening."

Robert knew her friend had just passed away and he sighed, "I'm sorry. I know you've been through a lot Laci. You shouldn't have to put up with me staying in the house too."

"No, it's fine. The more people in the house, the faster I'll feel better. I love having all the extra noise around," Laci smiled.

"Well I just stopped by to see if you wanted to have dinner but maybe it's not such a good idea. You look tired," Andrew whispered to her.

Laci looked at Andrew and smiled, "Thanks Andrew. If you want, we can order in some Chinese."

"Did you say Chinese?" Declan bellowed from the kitchen.

"Do you mind not eavesdropping like an obnoxious brother?" Laci bellowed back.

"Sorry but I'm hungry," Declan turned to Robert, "C'mon man they want to be alone. I'll show you the guest room."

Laci and Andrew watched them leave, "Be honest. You're tired."

"Is that a question or a statement?" Laci asked.

"Whichever," Andrew said, pulling her into his embrace. Laci wasn't sure how she felt about this but she did need some physical comfort. After finding about Kay, arguing with Amber, being suspended from work, and hearing about Declan' past, she needed some comfort.

"Laci?"

"Yes Andrew."

"I know things are really chaotic and you probably aren't in any condition to start a relationship with me right now but I want you to know something."

"Hmm?" Laci was snuggled up against his chest, her eyes closed.

"I'll wait for you."

Officer Tracy Stewart was looking at the photograph she had been given by Dr. Laci Cummings. It was of Dr. Cummings in her underwear and a sports bra. Scrawled on the back of the picture was a message that read, "Nice panties."

Officer Stewart sighed in frustration. She felt bad for Dr. Cummings. She looked across her desk at Officer Joe Bishop. He had been a jerk to Dr. Cummings and completely unprofessional. He was eating a tuna sandwich while looking at some files.

Officer Stewart curled her lip in disgust. "Hey Bishop!"

Joe looked up and Tracy could see the food in his mouth as he asked, "What's up?"

"You stink!"

He was taken aback, "I stink? No I don't I'm eating tuna."

Tracy got up and walked away from her desk. As she passed Officer Bishop, she whacked him over the head with a case file.

"Hey what did I do?"

"You've been a total prick to Dr. Cummings on her case. It needs to stop. If you can't be professional then I'll be more than happy to let the captain know."

"What gives? Why are you giving me a hard time all of a sudden because of Dr. Cummings?"

"Because she's a victim! She's going through a lot right now and I'm pretty sure it's more serious than whatever reason you've concocted in your mind to think she deserves your belittlement."

"Cut it out Stewart," Bishop shouted as she tried hitting him again with her manila folder.

"You've been warned," Stewart said pointing the folder in his direction leaving him to pick up the tuna sandwich he had dropped while she had been hitting him.

"Hey Laci, thanks for letting Robert stay here," Declan said as she was making a grocery list.

"It's not a problem. I actually feel safer with him in the house."

Declan laughed, "What are you trying to say?"

"Oops sorry Declan. I didn't mean to say you weren't man enough to protect the house or anything. I just meant, he'd be here as someone who knows security. That's all."

Declan shrugged, "It's okay. I understand. Anyway, I'm glad you let him stay. He's been through a lot."

"I thought him and his girlfriend just broke up. Was there more?" Laci asked.

Declan exhaled, "You know how I told you about my past?"

"Yeah," Laci said putting down her grocery list.

"Well Robert has been through something similar."

"Please don't tell me you two are secretly biological brothers!" Laci gasped.

"What? Stop acting like you're on a Spanish novella. No we weren't brothers but it's the reason we both became friends. Best friends."

Laci nodded, "Good."

"Good?"

"Yes, good. I'm glad you two found each other. I'm glad you two have each other to talk to."

"Anyway, thanks. That's all I wanted to say." Declan gave Laci a quick hug and went back upstairs. Laci finished making her grocery list. She wanted to keep her mind occupied since today was the day Kay was being buried. She would respect the wishes of Kay's parents. She wouldn't be selfish and upset them even more on a devastating day. She was going to make roast beef and eat dinner with Robert and Declan tonight. She grabbed her purse and headed out the door to go to the local grocery store, Publix.

Andrew was on his lunch break when George came up to him, "Are you still mad at me?"

Andrew sighed, "I'm not mad. I'm disappointed."

"Why do I feel like that's worse?"

Andrew wasn't sure what to say to George. He thought the entire situation towards Laci was handled inappropriately.

"Did you have something to say George?"

"I was just going to tell you that I talked to the bosses and they're okay with bringing Laci back onto the show as long as we can prove that she didn't send that photo."

"I should hope so, otherwise the station might get his with an unlawful termination lawsuit," Andrew muttered.

George blushed a little and cleared his throat, "Anyway, I'm hoping things get cleared up pretty soon." He was about to walk away when he turned around and said, "Oh yeah, there's a woman waiting for you down in the lobby. Security called up to tell me."

"Do you know who it is?"

George shook his head, "No, they didn't say. Just that she was upset."

Andrew didn't feel like being in his office without Laci so he took the elevator down to the lobby. He was greeted by an irate woman dressed in black, carrying a box that said, "Robert's crap."

"Can I help you?" Andrew asked.

"Robert told me that he moved in with Laci and Declan so I'm bringing you his crap," the woman shoved the box in Andrew's arms.

"I'm sorry. You are?"

"The name is Amber. I'm late for a funeral. Tell him I never want to speak with him again."

"I'm sorry. Amber was it? Why don't you take the box to him?" Andrew asked.

She gave him a bewildered look, "Are you kidding? So he can kill me?"

This threw Andrew off guard, "What?"

"Wow you're good looking, but you're pretty slow on the uptake aren't you doc?" Amber asked.

"Excuse me?"

Amber sighed, "Listen. I brought Robert's stuff here since I know you're dating Laci."

"You know Laci?" Andrew asked.

"Of course. We've been friends for a while. Anyway, that's Robert's junk. I was going to burn it but he got all crazy with me last night so I'm just returning it."

"What do you mean crazy?"

Amber lifted the long sleeve of her black dress and showed him a bruised wrist, "You see that? It's courtesy of Robert. I'm still pissed at Laci but tell her to be careful. He's a ticking time bomb."

Andrew watched the woman named Amber walk away and he looked at the contents of the box. Old photographs, books, and random items. Andrew was going to give it to a security guard to hold until he got out of work when a he accidentally dropped the box. He began picking up the items which included an old photobook. Some of the pictures had spilled out and he picked them up. As he picked up the last photograph, he caught a glimpse of the woman in the picture and cursed.

"You okay Dr. Brett?" the security guard asked.

Andrew stood up and shouted as he ran towards

the exit, "I gotta go. Let George know it was an emergency!"

Laci was looking at the carrots when someone called out to her, "Dr. Cummings?"

Laci turned around to see Veronica Watson Johnson, "Veronica?"

"I thought it was you. It's a small world," Veronica said softly.

"Hey I'm really sorry about the wedding. Declan told me everything. I didn't know. I'm so sorry."

"He told you everything?"

"Yeah. If I had known I would never have taken him along," Laci gave her an apologetic smile.

"How do you know Declan? Are you dating him?" Veronica asked.

"Eeew no. He's my brother."

"This is such a small world," Veronica repeated. "You said Declan told you everything?"

Laci wasn't following her but she was starting to feel a bit apprehensive, "Yeah. He told me how you two dated and then you dated his friend Robert. None of it worked out so it was probably really uncomfortable to see him at the wedding."

Veronica stared at Laci and asked, "Is that all he told you?"

"Yes. Is there more?"

Veronica grimaced, "I can't believe this. So you don't know?"

"Know what?" Laci was starting to get upset.

Veronica opened her mouth and in the middle of

the vegetable aisle, she began whispering to Laci exactly why she was upset during her wedding reception.

☐

CHAPTER 28

Laci was having trouble breathing as she pulled into her driveway. She looked at her house and took another unsteady breath as she exited her car. She was trying to process everything that Veronica had told her. She noticed her hand shaking as she unlocked her front door.

"Declan?" she called out. No one answered. She tried again, "Robert? Anybody home?"

The house remained quiet. Laci looked at the staircase that led to all the bedrooms and began climbing the stairs.

She thought of Veronica's parting words, "I'm not lying to you Dr. Cummings. Be careful who you trust."

Laci trusted many people. Andrew, Declan, Robert, Amber, and George. How could she think the worst of any of them?

She opened the door to the bedroom and peered in. It was empty so she stepped inside and looked around. The bedroom looked exactly as she had remembered it. A green and white comforter on the bed, a couple of boxes in the corner, and an empty bookshelf. She noticed a suitcase in the corner.

She looked around and rubbed her clammy palms on her pants before stepping over to it. She quickly unzipped it and saw…nothing.

"Why the heck am I listening to her anyway?" Laci asked herself.

She looked over to the closet. It was a walk-in closet with double doors. She opened one of the doors and saw clothing on the floor.

"Messy," she whispered to herself and was about to leave, when she noticed a small pink box in the corner. She thought it was odd and decided to take a look at it. She carried it to the bed and opened it.

She could feel herself shaking in fear as she lifted the contents out of the box. An instruction manual for a high-tech baby monitor, gold envelopes, and pictures. Pictures of Laci taken from the baby monitor.

"Impossible," she whispered. "I don't believe it."

"Why are you looking though my things?" a familiar voice asked from the doorway.

Laci spun around, "Declan!"

He looked past her to the pink box and frowned, "Who told you to go through my stuff Laci?"

She seemed taken aback, "Don't you know what I found Declan?"

He shrugged, "Pictures of me and my old girlfriends?"

"Yeah right. I found this!" she held up the manual for the baby monitor.

"Why are you showing me that?" he asked, a confused expression on her face.

"I found it in your box Declan. Tell me why it was there!"

"I don't know what you're even talking about!" Declan shouted back.

"You're my brother Declan! How could you do this

to me?"

"Do what to you?"

Laci was near tears, "How could you do this to me and my friends? Marie Ann and Kay!" It was at that moment that she realized she didn't have her cellphone.

"Laci, I don't know what you're talking about," Declan said, his hands in front of him defensively.

"Stop lying to me Declan! I met Veronica at the grocery store!"

Declan stopped moving forward, "Veronica? You met her? What did she tell you?"

"That you're a liar," Laci hissed.

"What?"

"You heard me. I know everything Declan. She told me that you were her abusive boyfriend. You!"

"And you believed her?" Declan asked, incredulously.

"Who else am I supposed to believe? You? My brother with a secret stash of stalker crap hidden in his closet?" Laci asked bitterly, tears seeping from her eyes.

"I'm not stalking you Laci! How could you even think that?" Declan ran a hand through his hair and sighed, "You shouldn't believe Veronica. She's a nut-job. She used to tell Robert I cheated on her and then she'd tell me Robert hit her. I almost stopped being friends with him because of her."

Laci didn't know what to believe. She loved her brother and up until Veronica made a tearful confession next to the bell peppers, she had always trusted him as well.

"Why is this stuff in your room, Declan?"

"I don't know. Maybe somebody put it there?"

Declan shrugged.

"Who could possibly be able to come into your room and hide this in your closet?"

Just then, they both heard Robert from downstairs, "Declan! Laci! I'm back!"

Laci gulped as she looked at her brother who signaled for her to be quiet. "I'm upstairs!"

They could hear Robert slowly walking up the stairs.

"I want you to run downstairs and call the cops," Declan whispered to his sister.

She nodded and they both waited for Robert to reach the top of the stairs. Once he reached the top, Laci ran past him, surprising him.

"Whoa, what's wrong?" Robert asked.

"She knows the truth," Declan answered.

"The truth?" Robert asked, not understanding what was happening.

"About Veronica," Declan insisted.

"Who?" Robert asked as he looked down to see Laci looking for her cellphone.

"Declan what the heck is-"His question was cut off as Declan pushed him. Robert lost his balance and stumbled down the stairs.

Laci gasped, "Robert!" She ran over to him and groaned. It looked like his neck had been broken in the fall. "Declan why did you push him?"

"I didn't push him. He fell." Declan calmly started walking down the stairs, causing a shiver of apprehension to trail down her spine.

"Declan, I saw you push him. Even if you didn't mean for him to fall, he's dead!"

Laci was having a hard time keeping herself under control. She wanted to cry but she was too scared.

"Where's your phone Declan? I can't find mine."

"Don't worry sis, I have your phone right here," Declan said as he pulled it out of his back pocket.

"What are you doing with my phone Declan?"

"You left it in your purse when you went upstairs to look through my personal belongings. Don't you remember?"

It was as if the world had stopped for Laci as everything seemed to make sense. She thought of Veronica's explanation of why she was upset. Veronica had said, "That guy you call a brother is abusive. He used to hit me and threaten to kill me. I trusted him and he abused me. You call yourself a psychologist? How can you not know that your own brother is some kind of sociopath?"

"No," Laci whispered as the thought of Declan being anything other than her sweet brother tore at her heart. "No!" she screamed louder as she covered her ears in hopes of stopping herself from hearing the thoughts that began playing through her mind.

Before he could speak, Laci shook her head, "No. I don't believe it. Is this one of your stupid jokes? Because it's not funny Declan." She could feel tears coming out of her eyes.

"Well I guess you figured things out. It's too bad Laci, we made a good sister-brother team."

"No! You're my baby brother! You're sweet and sensitive and you cheer me up when I'm sad. No! You cried when you ripped the wings off a butterfly. Remember? You couldn't do something like this."

Declan began laughing, "You still remember that butterfly? I wasn't crying Laci. I was laughing. Didn't you noticed that tears weren't coming out of my eyes?"

Laci took a step back and shook her head again, "No it can't be you. My stalker sent me a picture of you."

"I asked a friend to take a picture of me from far away. I was surprised you fell for that one Laci. I thought you were smarter than that."

"What about when you got that black eye?" Laci said as she began to slowly take another step back.

"I purposely hit my face on one of your stupid knickknacks. Laci are we going to do this all day? Ask me something good," he smiled at her and she shuddered.

"Something good?"

"You know…like why? Why did you do this Declan? Why?"

Laci was afraid she was going to start hyperventilating, "Why?"

"I'm so glad you asked," he said as if they were discussing something mundane like the weather. "I guess you could say I did it for revenge."

"Revenge?"

"All my life I've never had anyone love me Laci. No one. Not even my biological parents. Suddenly I got adopted and I have new parents and a sister. But I t didn't feel real to me Laci. None of it. I felt like a stray dog someone took in."

"What are you talking about? We loved you Declan. We all loved you."

"No!" Declan shouted, his face contorting in anger, "You pitied me! I have always had to look out for myself. I never had someone to look up to or someone that loved me back! I deserve better!"

Laci was horrified by his expression. She couldn't help but think he had gone mad.

"I tried to let it go Laci. I really did. I went off to college in a different state and I thought I could start anew. I thought things would be better. Do you know what happened to me?"

Laci didn't answer but took another step back.

"I met a woman. A beautiful woman. Her name was Daci and I thought she loved me. I thought, 'Wow, I'm finally finding someone who loves me because they want to.' It was amazing Laci."

"I don't remember a Daci," Laci whispered.

"Well Daci made a big mistake Laci. She cheated on me. So I had to get rid of her," Declan took another step closer to his sister.

"Get rid of her?" Laci asked.

"C'mon Laci! Stop acting stupid. Get with the program here! You don't have to be a rocket scientist to understand what I'm talking about."

"You killed her?"

"No her cheating killed her! I found another girlfriend I was serious about. That was Veronica. I didn't want her to cheat on my so I tried to keep her in line Laci. It's funny how they say it's a small world after all. She started listening to your show. Your stupid show where you spew love advice. She dumped me Laci. She left me all alone and I hated her for it."

"Declan, this is no-"

"Shut up! I'm not finished! I met another woman. Marie. I loved her too Laci but guess who she just loved to listen to on the radio?"

Laci stayed quiet, as she tried to figure out how she could escape.

"That's right! She listened to you. But this time I wasn't going to let her go. No one is ever going to leave me again Laci. At least not while they're breathing,"

"That's no reason to kill Declan! Other people break up every day!" Laci was starting to hiccup in fear.

"I don't care about other people Laci! I care about myself! I deserve someone to love me. Don't you understand that? I deserve it!"

"You're crazy Declan!"

"Well if it's coming from you it must be true."

She needed to buy more time to get closer to the door. "So why pretend to stalk your sister? That was your revenge? To scare me?"

"Oh no sis. I love you. You're the only family I have. I just decided to let you know what it feels like to lose someone you love. Why else do you think I pushed you and Andrew together?"

"You wanted me and Andrew to date so that you can break us up?" Laci took another step closer to the door.

"Not just that. I wanted you to lose your career. The picture to your workplace was a nice touch, wasn't it?" Declan began giggling and Laci could feel herself growing queasy.

"I loved you Declan. How could you do this to me?"

"Because you did it to me. It was destiny. Andrew suddenly began working on your show. He seemed attracted to you. I could feel the super power couple crap going on. I moved too fast though. You were starting to drift away from him because of the picture I sent to your workplace. I get that. Now that you found out the truth, that plan is all shot to heck."

"So now what?" Laci whispered.

"I guess I'll clean up loose ends. I found Robert killing my sister. I ran upstairs and he chased me. Then I shoved him away and he accidentally fell down the steps and broke his neck. I don't know what I'm going to do without my sister. I loved her so much." Laci was shocked by how genuine Declan sounded while he gave her his fake explanation.

"You really are insane," she muttered.

"And you really are a bad psychologist!" Declan advanced forth and reached for Laci who turned around to run out the door. He caused her to fall and he pulled on her ankle.

"Stop it Declan!" Laci was shouting at the top of her lungs.

"Say hi to mom and dad for me Laci."

Laci gave a final scream as the door burst open and Officer Tracy Stewart rushed, gun drawn, followed by Officer Joe Bishop.

The next few hours were a blur to Laci. She remembered Officer Bishop tackling Declan to the ground and arresting him. She remembered a paramedic talking to her. She even remembered Officer Bishop scrounging up an "I'm sorry."

"Laci are you okay?"

Laci looked at Andrew, who had his hands on her shoulders.

"Where's Declan?" she asked, looking around.

"They've taken him into custody Laci."

"It's not true. It can't be," she whispered in a quavering voice.

"I'm sorry Laci. Your friend Amber dropped off some of Robert's things at the office for me to deliver. I happened to see a picture of Veronica Watson, an old patient of mine. She was with Robert and Declan. Declan was kissing her cheek. I don't remember if I told you but she was the patient of mine that used to listen to your radio show. She always talked about her abusive boyfriend Nick. I didn't realize her Nick and your Declan were the same. I tried calling you but couldn't get through to you so I called the cops and we got here around the same time. They heard you screaming and they found you and your brother struggling. He's confessed."

"He confessed?"

"To everything. At least that's what Officer Stewart told me a few minutes ago when she called. Laci, I don't know how to tell you this, but-"

"He killed my friends," Laci said as if she were a zombie. "He's a murderer Andrew. He killed Robert. I saw him do it. It was like it was nothing to him."

"Laci, he confessed to two other murders."

She began weeping in Andrew's arms, "That's not Declan. It can't be Andrew. He's my brother. There has to be a different explanation. I can't…I can't deal with this."

"It's okay Laci, we'll figure things out. Everything's going to be okay."

"No it's not. Stop acting like you know when you don't know. You know nothing Andrew!" Laci continued to sob into Andrew's chest as he soothed her and kissed the top of her head.

Two hours later, Laci was sitting outside the police station. Declan had refused to see her. She didn't understand what was going on with her brother. She didn't understand how he could live a double life without her knowledge. Her job was to read people.

"Soda?"

Laci looked up to see Officer Joe Bishop standing

next to her. He had an arm extended offering her a Coke. She shook her head and he shrugged. He opened the can and began drinking the soda as he sat on the bench next to her.

"So...I've been a butt," Bishop said.

Laci didn't respond.

He continued, "At least that's what my partner keeps telling me. She said I should apologize. I did earlier but you were kinda out of it. So I'm saying sorry."

Laci held no expression. She felt numb, "You're apologizing because your partner told you to?"

"Yes. No. I mean...not really. I'm sorry I was such an ass and that I gave you a hard time. I'm also sorry about your brother. He seemed like a good guy. He made fun of cops but he was looking out for you."

Laci scoffed.

"When I was going through the Academy, we had to take a victims course. The instructor was some fancy psychiatrist. He gave us each two slips of paper and told us to write down the most horrible crime we could think of. I had too many to list. Rape...murder...you name it, I thought of it. I ended up putting down molestation."

Bishop looked at Laci who still hadn't responded to his story. He continued, "So anyway, this professor...he keeps talking and talking about what victims go through and how hard it is for them to speak up and stuff. We all totally forget about the pieces of paper until the end of class. He tells us to write down the name of the person we trust the most on the second piece of paper. Can you guess who I wrote?"

Laci still didn't respond. Bishop cleared his throat,

"I wrote down my father. He was a navy man. A good provider and role model. I remember feeling proud to be able to write my father's name as the person I trusted the most. Well guess what the professor said next."

Laci closed her eyes.

"Well, he said, 'Now that you wrote down the name of the person you trust most, I want you to imagine what you would do if you found out they committed the crime you abhorred the most? What would you do?"

Laci opened her eyes and looked at Bishop who was staring straight ahead.

"What would you do?" she asked in a low voice.

"I'm not gonna lie. I felt sick at the thought of my father doing something like that. I remember feeling doubt. There's no way that would happen. No way. Then I wondered what would I do if it was proven? Would I start hating him? He's my father. The man I loved and looked up to all my life. Maybe I couldn't look up to him anymore but should I stop loving him? I thought about it even after the seminar and I think I'd still love him. Not the bad side of him…but the good side. The side he showed me." Bishop looked at Laci, "I'm glad my situation wasn't real. My father never did anything horrible but I know what you're going through has got to be tough. I'm sorry it's happening. Your brother did some bad things. I don't really know why. A shrink is going to talk to him later. I'm sure you know all of this already but it's important to talk to someone if you're feeling upset. Don't hold it in. Even if your brother did bad things, he's still your brother. It's okay to still love him."

Laci didn't say anything to that so Bishop stood up,

"Okay well...I thought I'd just say that to you."

As Officer Bishop walked away, Laci called out, "Hey Bishop!"

He turned around, "Yeah?"

"Thank you."

He gave a quick nod and headed back into the police station to let Laci sit with her thoughts. Andrew came out of the station a few moments later, "Laci, he still won't let us see him. Are you going to be okay?"

Laci thought about what Officer Bishop had told her. She thought of her baby brother always cheering her up, making her laugh, and sticking up for her. He did bad things but there were still parts of him that were the Declan she knew and loved. Laci looked at Andrew and gave a weak smile, "I think so. It'll be tough...but everything's going to be okay."

☐

EPILOGUE

One year later

The newest article clipping was lying on the desk ready to add to the wall of news.

"Brother of Famous Love Guru Found Not Guilty by Reason of Insanity."

"He's not her brother! How dare they use that title for a woman who did nothing to save Declan. She even married the man who helped declare him crazy."

She put down her glass of champagne and picked up the latest newspaper and flattened it out carefully. Turning to the Celebrity News page, she noticed a picture not so much the picture but the heading.

"Dr. Laci Cummings and Dr. Andrew Brett Expecting First Child"

Her knuckles turned white with anger as she looked at a smiling Laci and Andrew while thinking of Declan locked away from the world.

"It's time for me to avenge you, my dear Declan. Laci never has and never will be a sister to you. She is let you get locked away from the world. Everything is going to be ok, though, my sweet Declan. It's time for someone to bring you the revenge you deserve. Your big sister is coming home."

ABOUT THE AUTHOR

L A Walton is the author of a innumerable books including children's and adult novels. She lives in Alexander City, Alabama.

Made in the USA
Charleston, SC
03 May 2016